NUMBERS FROM TEN

NUMBERS FROM TEN

HAREL SPENCER

PARTRIDGE
A Penguin Random House Company

ISBN: Hardcover   978-1-4828-3125-2
               Softcover   978-1-4828-3124-5
               eBook   978-1-4828-3126-9

Print information available on the last page.

To order additional copies of this book, contact
Toll Free 800 101 2657 (Singapore)
Toll Free 1 800 81 7340 (Malaysia)
orders.singapore@partridgepublishing.com

www.partridgepublishing.com/singapore

This is dedicated to

abcdefghijklmnopqrstuvwxyzabcdefghijklmnopqrstuvwxyzabcdefgh
ijklmnopqrstuvwxyzabcdefghijklmnopqrstuvwxyzabcdefghijklmnop
qrstuvwxyzabcdefghijklmnopqrstuvwxyzabcdefghijklmnopqrstuvwx
yzabcdefghijklmnopqrstuvwxyzabcdefghijklmnopqrstuvwxyzabcdef
ghijklmnopqrstuvwxyzabcdefghijklmnopqrstuvwxyzabcdefghijklmn
opqrstuvwxyzabcdefghijklmnopqrstuvwxyzabcdefghijklmnopqrstuv
wxyzabcdefghijklmnopqrstuvwxyzabcdefghijklmnopqrstuvwxyzabc
defghijklmnopqrstuvwxyzabcdefghijklmnopqrstuvwxyzabcdefghijkl
mnopqrstuvwxyzabcdefghijklmnopqrstuvwxyzabcdefghijklmnopqrs
tuvwxyzabcdefghijklmnopqrstuvwxyzabcdefghijklmnopqrstuvwxyz
abcdefghijklmnopqrstuvwxyzabcdefghijklmnopqrstuvwxyzabcdefgh
ijklmnopqrstuvwxyzabcdefghijklmnopqrstuvwxyzabcdefghijklmnop
qrstuvwxyzabcdefghijklmnopqrstuvwxyzabcdefghijklmnopqrstuvwx
yzabcdefghijklmnopqrstuvwxyzabcdefghijklmnopqrstuvwxyzabcdef
ghijklmnopqrstuvwxyzabcdefghijklmnopqrstuvwxyzabcdefghijklmn
opqrstuvwxyzabcdefghijklmnopqrstuvwxyzabcdefghijklmnopqrstuv
wxyzabcdefghijklmnopqrstuvwxyzabcdefghijklmnopqrstuvwxyzabc
defghijklmnopqrstuvwxyz.

All your fault

"don't panic." - Douglas Adams

Fore Words

To start you should.

Questions or statements are nuisances waiting to disagree. I am a will or a will not. Once famously not famous. I know that there was a famous day at least. Possibly a fifty year old man that pretends to be a Sherly on the weekends. That was surely. Or surly. Yes only on the weekends, I remember being a proud product of society. But then I have a question to Mark, what that was anyway. Not on the weekdays. Mark never took questions on those days. Those are work days. Probably are a were. I think I am not sure where the question to Mark goes in the week.

My week remembers the job that forgot all the weekly every days. Weekends are the perspective end of a week which every job should remember. When I think about it, I should remember it. Stand Ford is where I lived. I lastly saved the world sometime in 1997 preparing for a war back in the year 3000. Although firstly is what it would remember. My job, not me. I do not make this up, Strand Ford men never do. This is all real. None of this is made up. None of this is made up of real or make up. Only crazy people make things up. Good people have experience. Crazy people make up experience. Experience makes them both up and jobs make up nothing but time wasting forwards and sometimes backwards. The difference is a massive chasm of verbatim and perspective that can move mountains. My memories feel the same way as exuberance. The very same that all the one or the ones get out of a car crash aeroplane. They are ten, I think. Maybe more. But you have me here, I will remember trying and tell all the telling, much before 1997 and messiah complex. Back then in the future the voices lived in their apartment, not their heads. Only crazy people lived in apartments with voices.

Number 10

"There's a room, and in the room is a crazy man. He says: I am the walrus."

Frank Doz is a crazy crazy man

I saw a hospital. A ten story hospital, not the man kind, the animal kind. Possibly even the imagination kind. A low hi-rise. Not a store-y. We don't see the fresh sea air, but we smell it walking by. Back then I had all my apostrophes, grammar, and proper diction. I walk past the hospital every other day. My grammar sticking out for everyone to see. On those days between the every and other, I find a crowd. You can always tell what kind of crowds they are by the majority shirt color. Red for angry mob, blue for depressed, green for protest, orange for pride, etc…. You can tell this was sometime back in the year 2000, obvious. This crowd was purple. The dominant shirt shape was a cat-like. I have nothing to say about that. You ask the random person at the head of the crowd, close to the barricade: "What?" There's no point in finishing the sentence. "Dunno" would be the answer. The best kind of memory this was; came with other people's voices. The best of mental masturbation comes from crowds though. You ask the police shaped individual across the barricade, if you have a press-card (which I did, it was also the year 3000 and I was still fifty years old and back then I had my parentheses but lost some diction) that gets you through with some anecdotes, donuts, and answers. "Crazy man in ho-pital." Interrupted hearing is a selective blessing. Dropping letters from a

1

sentence also a selective blessing. "Crazy man ransom-ing ten story ho-pital." That sounds like a headline from a newspaper. "Crazy man is Frank Doz Jr." Who the hell is that? "Frank Doz Jr! A Big Bird on Sea Samey Strit." Frank Doz Jr. is a crazy crazy man. I use the card. I go up to the ninth story; the number ten found always offensive with clan oppression. I have to interview Frank Doz Jr.. Of course all of this was me looking for a hospital for my arm. Some time in the future I knew I would need to get a check up, so it seemed prudent to think ahead of the future, naturally. Only crazy men write their names with Jr. and then end the sentence without

Male Pregnancy is not a blessing

There is and was a Corona next to Frank by the window. Frank sees me, I see him, he sees my card. An immediate response would be a gunshot, but Frank was not insane, he was crazy with a gun dash (-) pistol. I speak to Frank Doz Jr., introductions and the sort. At that time I only needed to introduce myself, not my card. That would never need an introduction being already established in the mind of Frank Doz Jr.. He speaks to me, but first the card. He is angry at not me and also not the card. Of course at that time he was and not is, but I'm sure was an is too. But you see how this needs to be, not been or being. The imperative of the situation. Male pregnancy, he tells me, is not a blessing. A Big Bird cannot get pregnant. A Big Bird is the last surviving condor in the year 3000. He believes so I do too. I can see my card want to believe but is a little shy. He yells at me after that realization: "I can't get pregnant, CAN'T SAVE THE SPECIES, I COULDN'T GET PREGNANT! AND I DON'T WANT TO!" I can't tell if he can tell that I can't tell whether he can tell if he was or wasn't a real condor. Maybe he was at that point. He speaks about pregnancy not being a blessing, its painful. He's not sure whether he wants that much pain, even if it means saving the species. He says deforestation killed all the condors. I tell him they never lived in forests. He explains: "YOU, killing the forest, all the other animals move to mountains! I can't not think of an arc stuck on a mountain and all the hair I've lost during that conversation. Mother

Nature drops acid and lets it all ride, naturally not on the arc though. Naturally. The acid not the arc. The condors are muscled out, and now they're all dead. "AND I DON'T WANT TO GET PREGNANT!" he yells again, this time at my card which, in all honesty, owns me completely. On the 9th story, there's a bird cage next to a giant yellow condor head. We move across to the 8th floor, bad handwriting all around.

But Frank, I like cats!

I'm feeling a 1,2,3 aspect to this interview. Though, for the life of me, I forget how I ended up with this job in the first place. I like it. The job, not the forgetfulness my brain or memories, though even those are fun when you get a chance to talk and break bread with them. He says: "I like you" looking at my card. I don't like it anymore. The interview, not the job. The card, not the interview. He smokes a stick. Not a cigar, not a death dash (-) stick, he lights up a brown stick. He explains that death dash (-) sticks have five hundred and ninety nine chemicals in them. "Every time you smoke, release it all in the air. 599 chemicals." You can see him using his fingers to show the numbers, not speak them. Numbers are rarely spoken, unless in writing. They are rarely shown either. Always guessed. I ask for a brown stick, and I light it up. He explains that corporations will make their living on a poison they try on beings considered humans. He says: "Human Being humans, they become not living things until they have the currency". He explains that there's a reason they launched dogs instead of cats into space. I remember in a future year of 1976 it may have been monkeys. A coin toss and bad breath shot the dog into space and kept the cats grounded, monkeys stay in a future memory. Corporations tested the living grounded animals, like cats. I like cats. I say that to myself in mind dash (-) speak, almost certain that he heard it though. "Frank, I like cats" is what I actually say to him, which is why he heard it. Doubtful he could hear my mind speak in mind dash (-) speak. And that's all I can write about that. Billie Holiday sings in my head, A Big Bird head blinks at me from under his armpit, and the 7th floor comes up as we up to down.

The Devil in the satellite

I interest him in some UFO talk. "Do you believe?" I ask. "No. I can go blind" he says. He asks me to ask him to explain. I don't, but he does anyway. His breath smells like a man called Balimak, but he explains: "You look up, You look on TV, You stare at the pretty ladies. Death rays…satellites death rays, and you don't have to look up, just in front. For losing teeth you look at TV's. For brain cancer you can always dye your hair blond. Lunch cancer is a red." The hair of course, as he graciously explains. You can hear all the punctuation in his voice. He controlled precision, time, and my card's perspective. We go past room six hundred and sixty six on the 7th floor. The numbers are not real if they are not said in writing. He looks at me and speaks of a devil, a satellite, and a worm in an apple. You can see how everything in his mind is linked together. Talking to him was a smooth criminal sensation. Decatur is a very far off place, but the 6th floor is closer.

No more Automatic Flowers

"Frank, what do you think of automatic flowers?" I say. He looks at the cabinet full of honeycomb meds, "Great idea! Bees automatic sugar daddies!" The desert seems a better place than the 5th floor.

Speakup, I blew out my ear's drummer

You had to be there for interest. Not the kind of interest that weighs. Mainly the metaphysical kind that takes you in its stride. I was there, and I was swept off my feet by interest. She was as beautiful as she imagined me. I would see her in some distant memory of the future. Frank had an agenda and his agenda was not telling me much. Someone out there was not interested, yet. The 5th floor seemed perfect as all then numbers of five tend to do. Then a grenade kapboom. Less than perfect, scaring off all the numbers from the five. Another grenade with intent of kapboom. A third grenade with affirmation and more intent. Flash. I can't hear anything. Even my mind's claustrophobia gets claustrophobic. Or maybe it was the room spinning and it was my card. I can see Frank moving towards the staircase. He points to my attention and that very politely sees the 'no smoking' sign on the door. "SPEAK UP, I BLEW OUT MY EAR'S DRUMMER", not my response but I'm sure it was my instinct's. Sometimes they have a mind of their own. A song comes up and says, "Free Europe". There's a lonely American radio on the 4th floor not being bombarded by claustrophobic smoke.

We don't like fleas

He tells me with a yawn that he drives a hydroelectric car. Eco dash (-) friendly and cheap. That's in the year 3000, water and electricity have nothing to do with politics. Maybe it was the year 2000. For God & country…nothing else. Still hearing the punctuation and the ellipses. He tells me the headlights are cheap. Powered by morphine, foresight and a door's own morphine thoughts. His exact words: "God headlights, bad fleas. Morphine works to attract fleas. I don't like seeing fleas". I wish I had a Risk board to reason with him. The only time you reason with a mad man is when you are dividing up the world amongst yourselves. A man on the moon could be on the 3rd floor, instead.

Goats are not specific

He tells me he had house with one room and ten walls. He negotiated with these ten walls a peaceful existence. Scream operated, he was not the walls. Though he later changed that and explained it as the sliding doors that opened when screamed at. Still the walls were doing the screaming. "That's very interesting Frank." The same sweeping light of interest I had a while ago on some other number. It's a solar powered house. He's not a sun dash (-) worshipper, he thinks he can get good millage out of the house; all you need is the solar panel and a goat. "The goat, not necessarily required to be specific". The swinging door hits me in the face, I leave a goat stained red circle on the door. There's a point where you skip things. We skipped the 2nd floor, but there's the 1st.

A syringe to save the world

It gets boring. Not Frank, he is not an it. Honestly I don't remember
what gets boring. Maybe it's the lust for life. A why, is answered by a
shock. Though I only asked a what. He held up the hospital, ten stories.
He wants to make a statement, save the planet. Use a huge syringe
to suck out the CO_2 gas, pump it back out into space, or harvest it
to create a heat dash (-) shield. "How to do it Frank?" "I'll use A Big
Bird and the children. DON'T HIDE THE CHILDREN!" And he's
serious, now more than ever because I can't hear the punctuation. I
just fill in the blanks. I start walking towards the exit. No point in
staying here any longer. There's a will, there's a crazy crazy Frank Doz
Jr.. But I remember that males cannot get pregnant.

Number 9

"It's eyeballing the radio. There's too much to this that I don't know about."

In your life you have to make peace with the alphabet. Ever so often an a alphabet and less a the alphabet. There are seven specifics that you'll have to learn then. It took me seven days to learn these specifics, I hate them. I imagine a hamster that is truly gay. He is an alcoholic and a very reasonable one at that; the intrinsic reason that makes him a giant. Specials of kinds of hamsters. Radically he was almost two feet in height. There was a dash of white on his brown, a pirate's hat with a slogan, and a very confused looking skull sown in middle of it. The slogan never read what it sounded like. He never rhymed as good as the night, never procreated and was always almost sincere and out of sight. C(-)Charles was an it, the it was not talking, the talking never gave in, and it never liked the alphabet. No relation to the goldfish or the lion, these are promised truths after all. It had a specific and small etch(-)a(-)sketch board that never really liked it, the truth or the lion or the goldfish. That board was it's only communication method of communicating the communication. It was a communist with a love for "e". And then I remembered to start forgetting all the dashes. Effect of It's love for the "e".

I meet C(-)Charles outside of a bar in Franklin's century. That was a different places' time this time, away from all the Franks, the condors and the indifferent stories. There is a sharp point in the nighttime where different fonts start talking to you, they verbally abuse the dirt and treat you exactly like it. I was at that point, in Franklin's century. Outside the morning, smack in the middle of night, with almost no blood in my alcohol. We met, C(-)Charles introduces itself. The board itches and etches; you find on it a written death threat "your left hand will not be yours(-)e". The parenthesis do impress. You would think I would think this is the point that I lost my real left hand before it was replaced with a real fake. I am not sure. I figure that was a way of saying hello (it probably is, considering I still had my parenthesis at the time, I could feel it slowly dissolving into a baby step formula though), so I return the comment in kind saying "my left arm will be yours". My Franklin's century mind breaks into a song, there are dazzling lights, dancing divas, crazy bells, and three cows singing "Hello, I'd like to introduce myself and my names." The Captain of the SS period Enterprise. Saying that out loud causes confusion, C(-)Charles stared, rifled through a sentence on its board "I invented shampoo(-)e". Its at that point that my blood bailed, my alcohol took over and measuring cups were the highlight of the next morning. Sooner or later I would have lost my parenthesis and dashes. Later I would lose my question marks and feel the presence of a Mark.

Atrociousness(-)ness and the available(-)e

C(-)Charles etches the communist words on it's red board. The preaching itch burn through the etches. The diction of happiness, utopia, and benefit consideration present me with a gore(-)fest of a mindset. Not a glory hole mindset. That one has angel eyes. It tells me it has a boat's whale ready for me. In Franklin's century you get around through a boat (really all the world needed was just one boat), a boat's whale was a different grace of class. Looking a giant hamster in the eye throws all sorts of magnetic fields out of sync. Their impact on your face eventually result in eyebrows that share expression. The origin of brows to the eyes. In the end we all really share our eyebrows, there is only a few exclusive magnetic fields impacted by giant hamsters. Everyone knows that. You are sharing your eyebrows with me right now. We move out of the house, towards the actual dock, of course after we settle on who leads the eyebrows. The boat's whale was waiting for us. There was a Maybe Dick. Introductions were made; Maybe Dick was star(-)seeded. He was a Whale that belonged to a boat. You can hear the snare drum sail us away. The introductions of course were all left at the dock. I remember messy colors, lights, and a low of yellow. The first day was rough, not for the introductions by on the boat I remember. The lunch menu was horrific (I still had my diction back then). I was the only passenger that couldn't swim, I had one right hand at the time forgetting that the other was a left hand which may or may not have been a fake real. That was around the time my memory starting losing me. Perhaps not my real memory even. C(-)Charles captained the boat's whale. Maybe would only listen to C(-)Charles and C(-)Charles would not listen to me. My arm would listen to everyone though (the real fake realness), that's how I knew it wasn't really mine, probably. Naturally. Towards mid(-)day we spoke in questions. Where are we going? "Where E is available-e" What's E? "The E will help invent the radion(-)e". Are we eating soon? "Only when its available(-)e". It wasn't available till six days after. I was starved for sleep at that point and my hungry needed the rest.

Cautious optimism is required in the search for delicious(-)e

Maybe Dick tells me that we will be raiding land, and then he sprinkles me with the ocean's breath which you can see was too salty. This according to an ironically modest mouse that existed in dimensions of parallel. The sun looks for someone to worship it, in Franklin's century that was called heresy. But then I remember that Frank Doz Jr. was not a sun worshiper. They found a god and they kept to it. So did I. C(-)Charles asks me to prepare my left hand. At that point I would remember that my real not fake left hand is somewhere out there. It saw the disinterested micro(-)vacuum around me. It wasn't very happy with that, though that was never my fault. We hit land and it never fought back. There's a gypsy. C(-)Charles approaches the gypsy with cautious optimism. It etches a question "Do you have a break(-)fast(-)e?" The gypsy smiles, it presents food and speaks of how good it was eating it this morning with it's family. Maybe it said eating it's family. The vacuum did a job of goodness in keeping my memory of the future in check. C(-)Charles etches "In communism, we share(-)e." The gypsy takes us home. C-Charles asks me to go wait with Maybe. Some time later (a specific some time, not the usual sometime), it comes away from the house with a belly shaped like three gypsy persons. C-Charles listed cannibalism as a social expertise, asks me to help it get back on Maybe with my left hand. I lost interest, but my left hand gained it. I was my left hand's then. The fake real one.

Dire situations are a cancer(-)e

Denmark was raided, I gained nothing but my left hand found interest, the sweeping kind. Maybe Dick tells me they're coming after it. There's a cause to be won, a fight to be lost. He was trying to set an example. He leads me to a stash of brandy, I find interest again. The room dizzies itself while I get ready. My left hand goes numb as I start singing "a thousand miles away from home, there's a time to go and we need to go." Perhaps that was made up. The song not the memory. The memory stays in the vacuum with all the future present in the past. C(-)Charles jumps in the water. Eats a fish and a half. It tells me that there's a situation that I'm not aware of. There's a war coming. The It kind and Maybe's kind don't like. By eating fish it avoids cancer, to live and fight another day. I don't think it was fish that It meant though. Maybe people or future Pomegranates. By spreading the message it pollutes minds. Maybe's sailing his way through the ocean. We run out of brandy, and there are no more fish. Onboard again, Maybe tells me that he has a cancer and it entertains him.

Fredrick will invent narcolepsy(-)e

C(-)Charles etches away about his seven year old son. He ate him eight years after he was born. The son not the C(-)Charles. Fredrick he calls him. He's in France. We're in France. We're moving past French words. C(-)Charles etches "careful, don't think too loud(-)E". A family reunion later, my right hand is introduced to Fredrick's mother. C(-)Charles remembers cannibalism. Fredrick's mother has had enough existence, gracefully bowing to a tooth not in a stomach. The "e" is found under Fredrick's bed. We stay for a day; Fredrick never fell asleep. Surviving nine years into the future I can see he was invited on Maybe Dick. Even memories lie. But Fredrick was eaten before all that. He's part of the adventure. We will takeover the world I'm told.

Nauseous animals can be brutal(-)e

On board I invent drumming. Roll on the bass, there's a band playing onboard Maybe Dick and I'm leading it. We play songs about land, about the future's past, and about the present's paranoia. We fight only when Fredrick starts throwing up. Hamsters are not pretty when they throw up. Yellow on their white and brown does not mix. Fredrick was never really that, perhaps this too I made up. He gets locked in a cage. There's some saw in its base, he enjoys playing with it. He finds a match and starts a fire. Maybe that was me. Maybe was not happy with that, he dives. I see a fish underwater, it tells me to find purpose, a wasteland, a time box, and settle through oblivious broken glass. This ate up a good portion of the day; we never raided land in Europe after that. Europe made Fredrick nauseous.

Omnipresence is found in a radion(-)e

C(-)Charles beat everyone in Franklin's century. He created radion. I would find that the "e" was electricity. He put Fredrick to work in a wheel. Though at this point the more honest approach would be to say he put 'a Fredrick' not 'the Fredrick'. He ran through it, and the radion came alive. I stare at the box. It stares back at me with horrid noise in my direction. One day it will be the sole responsibility of a country to launch vacuum in space. My left hand kicks in and gives it the finger though, as it usually would do in most of these situation. C(-)Charles etches a sentence, Maybe Dick asks me to yell it at the radion: "Free the whales(-)e". Everyone heard that, everyone thought I was the voice of a god. You could see them all remembering what a god would sound like.

I'm not a fish you stupid man

Maybe speaks to me when we reach an America. I promise we were aiming for Europe first. There's a Columbus raiding off his boat. You can see him and his crew scurrying. Maybe Dick asks me to leave. Understanding decides to walk away from me. He tells me that he's not a fish. He's a wanted cancerous criminal. They will get him eventually, and then he will not exist. He tells me that fishing is killing his kind, because stupid men think he's edible. He decides to try eating men; if men don't stop eating him. I learned the specific. Left Maybe Dick, C(-)Charles, and Fredrick. On land I tell people that whales are not fish. No reason to talk about the eating part, to each his own. My right hand yells at me, my left hand goes back to being disinterested; we both know at this point it really isn't the real not fake real lefthand. I really had to find out who belonged to that left hand. They both eventually turn their back on me. The hands of course; I could see all their backs coming together with my head. That was not painful but painfilled.

—〜—

Number 8

"The bat's head found home on the ground, that was the worst minute of my life."

There's a South America in all of us. I've had a South America in me for as long as I can remember. Now my can legs shake for no reason, assuming they are mine. Its the precursor to too many things in my life and maybe yours. Making the point that my life is not yours. Possibly not even mine, but everything that happened in it was the true true and the closest thing I have to a run on memory in a sentence. You picture a brother meeting; and thats just what you get for eating a coconut. Some no(-)name corporation decides to have a promotion. What a party, a gift in each coconut. Inject a piece of paper and then theres too much fun. Paper has edges that cut. I learned that from a German some time in the past of a near future. Its a linear equation, and theres a gift. The paper, not the German. Field the equation and everything comes into play. Here's the Adam of a West, the Batman of his age, a hero of some distant television hour that passed and past.

In the Adam of a West is one thought. "Go to Gamba". European thoughts are left in Europe, but you should always spread them when you have a radion and the secret of saving the universe. When you aim for Europe you end up in America though, and at the end of it all never save the universe. I did though. He was obliging. "We're going to South America! I know this great prophet; he speaks in tongues

17

and sells great togas!" Theres an old(-)man blinking his face without sunglasses, envy of the crowd. Theres a seven continent feel to Adam's words. "Go to Gamba" and then Batman crashes a homeless aeroplane for homefull people through the right side of a mountain. Air travel has always been preferred. All the fucking time.

Crash one signal A

The train wreck question, where is Antarctica? Right there and there's a white hummer obese(-)Lee blocking my pointing finger. You can see his back side from his front. Here is Antarctica Adam. And Adam shrugs my sentence away from his ear and says "here's the Gamba". Adam was Batman, he has inclination to befriend animals, but not kill them. Of course at that time I say has, but it really was had. Even Adams had and have feelings. Theres a beat to his step, we walk through a glacier which on its day sunk the Titanic. "Here we are then, heres a penguin, I'll call him Patrick" Adam speaks to the penguin but means to log that sentence in the ledger which was my face. Hollywood stars and their imaginations. Cute. I have issues with penguins and the color blue. You can't ever wear blue when you're in Antarctica. Patrick has the assaulting air of a ravenous ass. Sort of like Lee, which I am no longer sure was real, as real as my fake real left hand. Maybe is not here now. He doesn't speak to me but Adam tells me he speaks to him, Maybe. It's mothers day and all the penguins are buying and selling their mothers. There seems to be a shake in my hip but Adam's is stable. There's a song in my ear, but Patrick is deaf. He's a magical penguin, that's what Adam tells me. A one spouse penguin, never playing with fidelity or the 'in' part of it. Patrick teaches Adam how to love and cherish his right hand which I later came to know discovered the color red and became my fake real left hand. The Antarctic sun beat it to a pulp and now it's red. Or maybe it was the Arctic. We leave Antarctica the moment we crash the sled of a trip that I cannot remember. Even penguins can't drive (that much I know and do not need to remember), and then there's a marriage proposal from Adam to his red right hand. The matrimony night celebrates the union and we leave, with Adam now legally married to his red right hand, for now.

Crash three four skipping two

Theres an abysmal sensation that I get when I sleep. But I never did sleep. My right hand tells me there's nothing to it, but every time I think is bullshit. At that point my brain did not think in shit, a different kind of language developed by the late tribe of (fill in the blank). Knowing the future in the present I realise my lack of sleep was due to a fornication between my real left hand and the fake real left hand. The fake real left hand was always on top. In Australia you find no horses, only left hand fornication. Adam befriends an aborigine, his name is Susan. He sings like an angel, thinking to all of us that he comes from the land down under (do not fill in the blank), the real land down under (again no need to fill in the blank). Susan trades all the gold for very little bread, he sleeps on a spring and chessboards across time. Adam asks him about the Gamba right before he sleeps. There's a desert answer to his question, it's out there with a pointy smash, smoke, and a lot of talking bears of a gummy nature with chickens and a Lola. Here's the laugh that Adam speaks, a high squeak pitch(-)less laugh void. We discuss the potential of expansion to other continents. He tells us that kangaroos are not allowed to expand. The moment they're displaced, they really are a handful. Susan's friend is a kangaroo (never a pet, still having my parenthesis at the time), it moves through the range but not through time. It springs to life with half a smile. I never knew kangaroos could smile, this one could sing too. There's no mothers day in Australia, theres a concert by kangaroos though. Adam and his red right hand insist to go, still not becoming my fake real left hand. "Thats that Gamba!" and I'm convinced. Register the thought and theres a heaven behind it. Theres a mole digging under the concert ground, it wants in. The mole is out. The mole is angry. It digs through and the stage crashes. I crash on the spring, and I fall off it. I see blue. I hate sleeping, Adam yells at me for saying "h(-)a(-)t(-)e". If I spell it he won't hear it. His red right hand doesn't like to hate. Batman fights the moles, pretending Superman never existed.

Crash five breaded functions

Smash and heavy(-)up the function, the elevator then comes to life. Adam West married his red right hand for money. That makes sense. It is a year that feels like 2011 and everyone's living in a weighted century of only averages. Theres a starved man standing next to a loud sound "Go to the India and ride the elevator". We're told that there's a magic elevator, it feels, it eats. I waited, Adam waited, his red right hand's done now standing alone in a corner (even red right hands find a convenience to pissing in parking lots). "The elevator has the Gamba", but I tell Adam that first we need to find a troubled elephant. I know where we can find one; he can read between the lines. Elephants shouldn't be killed, in India there's a whole (not hole) people that think they're some types of gods. Not just one elephant, all of them of course. Again with a linear feel. Finding the elephant was never a hard thing. Finding one with jeans big enough was a tough action to remember. Maybe it was genes, not jeans. I found the elephant eating a tiger, in 2011 mother nature owns a blackened berry and forgets. I work the elephant with a drum (the same my drummer lost) AND you can see Adam dancing to it from your seat in the present. Crazy man. No dogs follow us, and into the Asiatic magic elevator we go. Though I am not sure we ever did, not this time. The elevator slides the door with a happy sigh, the nod to a Douglas Adams past. Knowing well this may not be true. The elevator likes my drums (the same ones I lost and never had), it asks me to play the beat (tap tap tap tap tap tap). I walk around the elephant and Adam as he makes out with his red right hand. I would never do that. I press three buttons and the elevator door opens right where the elevator door stops. There's nothing outside but a sign that says "Ivory Coast for sale". Maybe it was meant for chocolate or cookies. There's a deranged old man selling countries at the top of the mountain. He was smelling them before he sold them too, I remember that truth too. I try to get out of the elevator, the cable snaps and the door closes. I really don't think there ever was an elevator. A free(-)fall meets happy music. The happy music cushions the free(-)fall, and Adam flies out with his red right hand, he grabs me with his left one and we make it through the night. Theres a hero, even in Batman.

Crash seven at a mile per hour

There was an explosion and vegetables took over South America. Not the south of America. There's a man pretending to be the ruler of South America, his name is Trugadore. He left his wooden eye next to his real one, they stole it and he couldn't see. Asparagus pushed him off the chair and then Carrot walked up to him and punched him in the stomach. He says that knocked him out of his conscience, living in it as all rulers of nations tend to do. Adam leads the conversation as the lights try to go out. He looks at the ceiling lighting, and his red right hand waves itself, you can tell its yelling insults. There's a buffalo waiting to sit in our table. It flies over with its magically colored wings, flaunting the fact that it has access to radioactive labs. This was before I had an assistant. Adam ignores it. Not my assistant, the butterfly. I can't ignore it, its breathing down my neck. The Gamba, Adam tells me, is down the sewer, up the antsy hill and through a rainforest, now exclusively growing carrots. Not Carrot, Tigger or Pooh. "Go got the Gamba" he tells me as we're getting ready to get up. On the bus down the sewer, I tell Adam that I need to be sure. The last shadow getting on the bus told me so, it was eerie. As I do not now, I had some control over my feelings. Adam's left hand slaps me; his red right hand then asks me to compose himself and reaches for his belt. Adam remembers Batman and the utility belt. If only he was with me on the aeroplane. Clearly I'm his Robin. There's an angry bus driver in the seat next to me. The bus slips and tips over into the water, some vegetable decided that it would be funny to leave a rope around the bus's wheel, in case someone go too close. A gremlin for a Batman.

The nine fingered hand

There's a break in Adam's sentence. We're riding the bus's left front wheel through the sewer. Into the rainforest. Expectations of truth. The red right hand points through the same white hummer. At that point I see that it had nine fingers. The red right hand, not the man. Finding a man on a chair behind a desk, which I later found after noticing the fingers on the red right hand. Theres a little plastic plane on his desk. The plane has the word Gamba written on it. Finding the Gamba, Adam of the West cranks out a red right hand punch that throws the man off the chair. He then says to him and the floor next to him "plane exhaust is killing the ozone...way too fast. Because of your Gamba, all the bats are dying". Batman helps me fly into the year 3000, later on in the past and gives me his right right hand complete with a finger numbered 10.

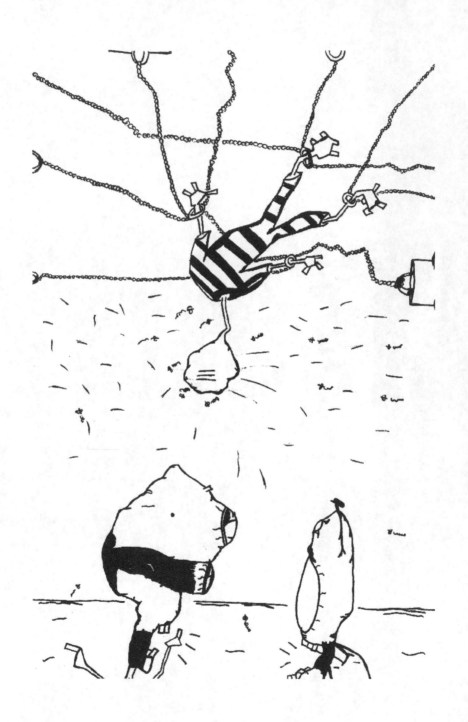

Number 7

"Here's the white(-)man music. Its devilspeak."

Everyone talks about hero situations, rarely is there room to discuss these points and their returns in amusement parks. Mix it up with schizophrenia and it all becomes a near complete shadow of enjoyment. Its meek and modest for all you care, but worry about nothing. It never comes for you, it always will. It's usually the person behind you. Most often it is you. They fly helicopters and escalators, the people behind you. And then there's always the person behind you tomorrow. These people you can never tell, they're more likely to be synaesthetic. Theres another point to this, is that person aerodynamic? They're qualified to fly helicopters, but can they fly? You wait and say things, but these things leave you behind and they already said you. And you never hear them but they have always heard you. Clearly Mark was not introduced to them.

Supersonic Indians make the best airport workers. They're fantastically aerodynamic too. Every individual comes equipped with a bi(-)polar disorder. Their jobs are simple, its about them falling apart everywhere. In relation to aeroplanes they use themselves to balance the engines, like cartoon clowns on real aeroplanes. One half of a bi(-)polar disorder on each wing, that makes the plane go "WHOOO WHOOO WHOOO" (even aeroplanes get excited and panic). Theres a poetry happiness to them, no care in the world, but maybe thats the individual they are at that moment. On the other hand you can picture them being the progressive individuals that no one cares to hang out with in party situations.

In the month of a September

Only darkness remembers how the land was before the light. Theres a special stylized dance for pieces of land that were that barren. Void of light naturally. I couldn't avoid something as flat, too flat, and irredeemably flat as that. The piece of land was not too big and not too small. Big enough to hold ghosts that liked girls (not in aeroplanes though because ghosts have a very strong fear of flying); it would have been almost a football field's size if it had decided to be a football field. Then there was Ghandi's brother in the airport. Theres a flight that I've been always meaning to catch, but the shuffle to the terminal was too much for me and at the time for my left hand which I was sure now is mine. I caught him instead in a month where a progressive individual's purpose was to balance an aeroplane. Theres nothing to lose he tells me, it never gets too much because he is always never paying attention. The pay is good (never for the attention, you will notice I still had my parenthesis then), but he believes that theres a higher order destiny. I tell him about the land and how it was pretentiously avoiding being a football field with light. He considers it a term of human endearment, the pretentiousness. He tells me something close to a life; he calls it the life of Ryan. He is looking forward to something, this Ryan; he wants his own amusement park nothing related to his brother. Maybe he was not Indian after all. He wants something to lose, an amusement park thats completely clean and green. His old man discussion ends with your typical TV episode ending, roll on the credits and the music hits the scene with violence and prejudice. The aeroplane decides to land and my seat yells at me to take the stewardess and buckle her belt up.

The Oddball Jack and the month of November

The hero of that time, Ryan, Ghandi's brother, quits his job. He packs his things and decides to embrace a higher order of a pointed view with a racist drum of a thunderclap. Roll on new credits, theres an idea brewing. There is if I were thinking of that time, there was if I was remembering it, it probably happened in the future's distant present. I don't barren walks but did barren the land for a walk and at the same time he takes me through his blueprints. He is not looking to build humans, but he shows me abjection and objects similar to their color. It is about imagination and how often rides can create mobs of people. He did ride my imagination at this point, or will. He wants to build the world's tallest escalator, make it seem like its crashing and call that Fun (with capitals because they sound better). He thinks of a thunder based game, a cubical room with nothing but an electric hum and accordion to play. I did share with him my plans for a radion but that never impressed him. You're electrocuted if you don't play the right notes, but it's an equalized zap linked to an accordion that at a closer glance would look like a very alive piano. That, he calls Entertainment (also with capitals because that is an attractive word when capitalised). The bear cage is a suspension of a cliffhanger ride. It is an inflated yellow boat in the shape of a submarine that did look like a taxi if you let it. None of the land's pretentiousness there. He will suspend that over bears, and there's a goat involved to foreplay the bears. He calls that the Laughing Mat(-)ter. Not to be confused with a laughing Matt which is locked somewhere in a joke of a horror house. He shows me drawings of his mascot; a blue and white goat called the Oddball Jack. The rain drives a hard bargain; his bi(-)polar attitude does not balance the weather as well as it balances aeroplanes. The institution pages me back, I have my fingers answer their call, but I never really pay attention, I have to leave Ryan with intention that wants to have a nice day. The fingers on my left hand finger air fingers at a trumpet.

The Irish Goat uprising of January

The world almost came to an end many many times. The Irish had little ambition to overtake the takeover; their goats decided that maybe they should run it instead. There was a war, I had to cover that (again thinking I was part of a pressed press of a pressing), I had to run away from a goat while wearing a bell too. I spent substantial currency time in their camps, too much time in the open grasslands of Ireland. There was too much green to the red, and my eyes decided that it was almost about enough. I left through a balance(-)less flight to Heathrow. I land and I go meet Ryan. His bemusement park is open, Ryan's World, his Oddball Jack was, did, and is greeting me. You say hello through a strategic left hook to the face. Goats are known to go to hell, but they'll take you with them. Our hero fortifies himself in his amusement park, it is the greenest amusement park by far, no carbon footprint, no luxurious food, just tofu and all it's pretend splendour. None of this was in the institution, maybe it was. Really emphasizing the real. Oddball Jack is a soulless coat without Garth. Garth wears Oddball Jack, and Garth likes to touch all the pink nipples. All located on the suit of course, sexual harassment does not belong in an amusement park, Angy. You are supposed to punch Oddball Jack (and I swear I did), I discuss punching Garth in the face with Ryan, he does not object, he shows abjection towards him as well. There's a punch in the face and Garth decides to be something of a traitor masturbator. It is a new year and Ryan's World is betrayed by Garth. I think Garth was made up by Ryan. Maybe I was as well.

The Passion of the Garth in good March

I had Garth in my sights; we locked him up in the Entertainment. The goats were everywhere by then. They closed down all intention of communication between Ryan's World and the outside inside of the rest of the world. We had to make do with tofu seasoning for everything; it's the healthiest deadly period I've ever had to go through. No meat consumption for six months (as all the no ones will remember). Garth thought his paternal unit was a goat for a dad. The Oddball Jack suit suddenly held more meaning to him than anything else in the world. He threatened and beckoned for nuclear disaster. Ignorance. All the no ones knew at the time that nuclear disasters openly discriminate against goats and all their pretends. Ryan would speak about how a nuclear disaster would kill the goats too, thats how I knew that. He had little sense at that stage, his accordion playing fingers messed up and the amps of electricity would help correct that. Not even radion could fix that. Maybe the accordion was in his pockets. It is an over and over process.

Good night and good luck Entertainment in May

We were still holding out when Garth ran away. He thinks the goats broke him out. He thought that the goats thought that he was a divine think thought. Gods don't entertain thoughts of thinking nipple squeezing men. Men cannot get pregnant said the condor in Frank Doz Jr., very naturally too. The goats, they just weren't able to stand the white(-)man musik. The bemusement park had little power left, green generators were never meant to run on an empty six months full of tofu and institutional coup d'states. Garth broke out of Entertainment, and Entertainment blew itself upwards with no one to play the erect accordion. Ryan was not happy. Even he couldn't balance that shit out.

The Suitcase Nuke of July

You have and will broker a truce with the goats. They surrounded us for too long. We had no food. We had no bad intentions, not in the light of day anyway. The tofu was the real hostage taker though, I forget to remember that this time. Perhaps it was a tofu god they were looking for. The goats naturally, not us. Trying to feed them green onions didn't work. Ryan and I opted for pilgrimage. Ryan's World would be destroyed. Garth carried a suitcase nuke, which the goats blew upwards with him attached as he walked in Ryan's World. No more nipple touching Oddball Jack and thoughts of a ford for ungodly amusement. Ryan goes back to his aeroplane job. He picks up an umbrella later on which I see had made him it's bitch almost instantly. The airlines welcome him back, with all the ash on the ground and fallout in the air, aeroplanes could not fly without supersonic bi(-) polar progressive Indians. Ryan's World was the first and only green amusement park; it was not a gay amusement park. Oddball Jack met people in it, but Oddball Jack was also killed in it by tofu worshipping goats. I leave Ryan with nothing but a hello. He tells me that he wasn't bipolar, he was schizophrenic. Apparently, you're only schizophrenic when the voices inside your head repeat themselves. A friendly tofu(-)less god of a renegade. I take one of the voices from him, very later and soon it becomes my assistant. And some time after that it becomes you Angy.

Number 6

"Quickly now, COIL the Flashyst wearing number fourteen!"

On a field of green I exclaim to my assistant that everyone should be able to burn down houses. Jealousy points and in the insane righteousness demand such things to happen and be done, executed. My assistant, short and looking like a blood clot wearing a sailor's time ruptured suit, takes out a box of wary matches. I now find an assistant in what would have been an Indian's schizophrenia. Of course that was then. He would be a blond sounding jungle book prancing around a fire, I took him in to make him human. Then then, not the now now. Of course. Back to the then, white and blue strips, count one, count two, count there, three. Matches are cranky, not burning. Tonight is my birthdate, my assistant wants to light up the green field, and it would be my birthday cake. There is a lonely wolf in the field, fur messed up, grey and insane looking. The wolf not the fur. The fur being an extended aura of the wolf. The wolf is chased by my assistant. A blood clot runs after a four legged un(-)blood clot, woof woof. Words are thrown all over, matches are happy ever nevers. Words, unlike paper, are blunt but have sharp edges, similar to ideas. There is no such thing as a word cut, I thought to think. The field of green lights up, happy day, birthdate lightning and lighting. My assistant finds a seat for a pet to keep. Thinking backwards and you can and would see the seat thinking my assistant was it's pet.

Shifting the Sean Connery

"Continues bossie. Yah asee that is ok." My assistant was a Danish Queen of a thought, royalty. "Bossie, Aaron had to go. Left hem year oft last. No good, killet zee animals, could nat trafel to cranky moon." All end sentence periods belong in quotations. We were in an Africa. Maybe it was Africa, but definitely I often never mistook that for a Southern America. It looked nothing like the moon, or an anvil. His plan was to go to the moon, friends and all. His Aaron saved up a trusty(-)fund. A shaved trusted fund, later with no doubt, speaking to me he cries. His Aaron killed the animals. He wanted all the elephants dead. The elephants that had nothing to do with movies. Aaron was code for the Sean Connery. Hollywood is obsessed, the Sir Sean Connery, spankingly good in something, not very in much of a lot of other things. Obsession with ivory, killing elephants thinking ivory is a substitute for Adrenalin. Stuck(-)up superstar, hunting elephants and kicking babies through moon pies. Bad man. Elephants are off(-)limits, exactly what I said some time ago in the future. "Could nat keep reel. Mayjor man proplem." the Sir Sean Connery sees fantasia in elephants, dancing and sneezing. Stubborn cello plays when he sees elephants. Runs after them pretending to bite at them. Really just wanted their tusks for a quick fix. Maybe it wasn't elephants, probably a rhinoceros, but I would imagine then they were elephants, even the rhinoceroses. Hollywood stars peddling ivory, it was the is and new smack. But that was them some time in the present I would imagine to remember. My assistant gos on to rant about the future of smack Ivory. The high he gets from ivory, tusks. Bit by a mosquito, dry tank in the beginning, towards the end flies away with a top off and a tip too. "Pulling babi elefants by tails qyesshun to Mark. Nat fun." My assistant cursed him, black voodoo magic, derived from a none Southern America. Window shades down. The Sir Sean Connery flies over to his Nevereverland. His brain brain finds something new, Scottish accents and their inherited sexiness. My brains only find Mark, flirting to eventually start asking all the questions.

Cooking Colonel Saunders Sanders

What about Cherry flavored lies? "Nay bossie. Chicken man knok on doors making Lola, whyte klows, and whoness. Tells of tyme ant beginnings to people. Yalls to people on chickenz and jaily gummy pears." Answering the door and finding a cooking Sanders, a kaleidoscope of towers hits you. You see dark shaped rainbows; the man glows and presents you with what looks to be diamonds, real glossy chickens. The disaster of the ages, fried food, was not incurred. Picked it up and ran with it, strong motion and the sense. Sexy in times of horrific. Tells you lies in the newspapers, Sanders laughs and drags your head into a white cloud, convincing you that glossy hue of chicken is really the right way to go. "Too mach boison. Pichurez and all bossie. He lyez. She hearz lyez and believez." No electricity in most of these houses, Sanders advocates his glossy hue chicken and makes a beatnik profit. Shankly is the brand name for glossy chickens. Never ask where they came from. "Women Lola marriez Chicken man. Thoughtz his love bee trew." Shelf life and expectancy usually is limited, half(-)life ranging dangerous and very poison (intentionally avoiding the poisonous). Glossy hue chicken slowly eats away the proteins in your body. Reflect on their osmosis, it never exists. Dances in all your Nancies and then a body of making. The natural progression is belief in a just cause. Leave it alone and you develop a major case of bitch(-)tits or manly's(-)boobs. "I feedz Chicken man. Glossy whoness chickenz make him crasy. Crasy man, crasy woman. Tyme to leave." Sanders is a man that wanted to sell a world to another world's world. Finds a magic harp, rubs it the right way and a piano voice plays him out across a disheveled head of a beach. That was the future of aerodynamic chickens. Starts his own business, something with major secrets upgrading from a Colonel secret. Ingredient that never had ivory, all fifty spices and glossy hue chickens. It leaves you up in the air.

An Arnold Schwarzenegger Jr.

Spinal adjustment with a glass libido and adrenaline fixation, horse(-)like man. "Mr.Bik man never cry. His moonly gods. Bik akscent. Plaiez gamez with metalz. Bik Man, no need, but Mr.Bik man getz bikker." He starts his own brand of medicinal fatness, amino acids and the like. It really likes people, especially those that like it. People that are puppets for other people, not able to bite, sneeze, or heal properly. People are made to heal in the eventuality of time. Even blonds. "Durty shoez all tyme. Liked he waz Mr.Bik man. Selling to horzez. Horzez take all medisin. Like to take medicine, openz windowz for all horzez. Make all Bik men, like Mr.Bik man." Trains think they can stop a man, man thinks he is a horse that can stop a train. Horses never liked being dragged into this. Industrialization kicks in, so does self awareness. They see spots, colorful fantasy shaped spots and they runaway from home. The gods of all small chicken wings. Insecurities take over, body mass and the like revel the opportunity. Hot sun blazing on foreheads and they faint, the gods of small chicken wings of course. "Mr.Bik man sellz lyez tow. Never tellz all real. Tellz haugh real. Peoplez never tinker better." Trains under the sun never think twice, the horses nod their way into historic forgetfulness. All time is kept in a pink box at the end of a timed rainbow. Horse(-)like men, very big men, think twice. Too much anger, testosterone files high. Wars break(-)out. People find a reason to be happy when they're miserable. "He givez memoriez tow. I do nathink." Big men move to Kathmandu, Tibet, and Kurdistan and all the horses grabb the first train out. No venom, just testosterone and conflict. Great combinations waving down, up, a fire with good intentions. Fire(-)up the wood(-)saw; hide under your desk, there really nothing you can do that has not already thought it could be done.

Jacqueing a Cousteau

Diving for a woman's interest. "Watershaman good man. Likez woman. Digz deep in waterz. No wyind in waterz, holdz too much in. Nkow boom on the inzide." Soft shock and it is a blitz on your internal organs. You wake up one morning finding out that you spent a good portion of your life not on top of water, whether in a glass, womb, or under a glass in a wombing bathroom. Dream of something like fish, fish that you'll see you only once in their twice lives. Imperative action, sleep now, rest. "Hiz zmile for Angy. Angy he liked much, digz deep deep all time to find preshiouz. Findz glossy thingz. Tellz people no can takez. Peoplez no lizten." Theres a glad all over feeling in Mr. Cousteau's ambition. His waltz with the devils shows off a lot of scars on his knees. Though I see happy reasons to not do what he would do in the past future. Even fish know better than screwing with a man on a mission, especially a boat's whale. Angy liked him, he liked her, but she liked shinny things, materials. "I azk him, looking for qyesshun to Mark. He foundz. Foolish, he grinz at me". Angy turns, tells everyone of the shiny dimension of the sea. People dig deeper than Mr. Cousteau. It all started with foolish grin, the fish did mind. Perhaps only when in the imagination, that was the only safety. They don't like the flash. It was an is now or never occurrence. A failure in disarming the racing underwater bomb that is aquatic deforestation kangaroo boxing or donkey dialogue. No more demanding precursors. "I advice him. Forgetz Angy, other fish in the zea." I keep him around for his cute words, they can read me.

Camp fire grows dim. Chairs are picked up and asked nicely to corner. People on the chairs are then casualties of a day's lost war. It is a was revolution today. It is my birthdate. The man wearing number four and teen is a classy fascist. Black jersey, very white skin, abnormal concurrence and an Iron Lion Zion playing in mind. My assistant points my attention to the ass burning the grass. The wolf ran away, my birthdate present. My back(-)up birthdate present is a singing ass, damaged and stripped. In Africa, zebras, asses, can be set on fire. "You are Sebra man." Maybe he did say that. It was all about my need to robot smack the electro gear. Or was it electrogear, you would look to Mark. I have no electrogear and a very healthy karate chop. Zebra's next. Ka(-)pow!

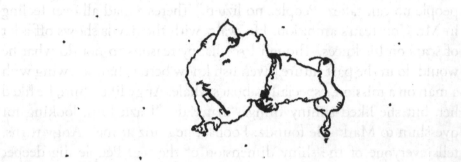

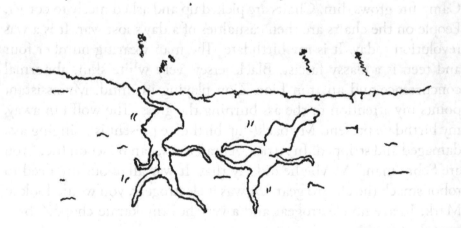

Number 5

"Angy tick ticks...it does not mean I am there. Questioning Mark."

This is me being the corner. I'm being me in the corner too. You're being me being you in the other corner. Why are you being me in the corner, question to Mark. They're being me being you being me, so really being us, in the other corner, right center left of all the others pretending to be one and not the other. We're called the misfits, as was the right terminology somewhere back in that time in the future. The desert treks were and are and continue to be good for walkabouts, especially when looking for time travel. Your good mood plush and ripe with redundancy and an angry Philippine native manwomen, asking for monetary compensation for service of formaldehyde, urinal cakes, and recognizable cists. A known fact that the Philippines perfected time travel and owned all the rights to it's walkabouts. My good mood running away, get the tranquilizer gun and shoot. Deadliness for the Philippine time travel police. A Ray Bradbury nod. Fat man in the desert looking twice at temptation, but no tattoos to tell stories. Angy, you'll take the scissors and run with them towards that man, and tell him never to cut down thunder, zinc mines, and trees. Man comes from the land down under Angy, that's the same country France tried to takeover, requisition. Angy judo chop his ass. But Angy, this would be the point that you pose the question to Mark, question mark. My assistant would have been proud.

Nuclear bombs sing about young men dying, the desert sighs and nothing comes from that, never again. Excessive use of apostrophes always preempts not using any periods. Here is where we are an Angy, that door is not real by the way. Honest. You need to question Mark. Stay away from that door, it is tearing me inside watching you slide up and down like that Angy. Who is Angy, question to Mark. We will find a way to start out. Starting to do lies now. Your idea to make a stand, it was the owned chapter of a yesterday but you had to stick to it. Shall we try again, question to Mark. Is your cell(-)phone working Angy, question mark. Here is my wine, I made it yesterday using a water filter, and here we are through the desert with lights pretending harmless thoughts, what fuckers, she thinks without the use of the usual grammatical correctness. Maybe that was me. I believe in asterisk thoughts though. In a suicide college, kids are taught to teach, running around indoors and killing time outdoors. The weather plots with time to kill, all failed. Question to Mark. Cells divide, mitosis, Canada comes across as harmless for only snow and all species of trees. Long desert walks are the case of fall(-)out in an escaping population. A walk about dream waking up across an Africa meant to have been Europe but turned into a Southern America. All this and Asians discovered walkabout time travels. They only drove on the right in those lanes.

Do not blame the VCR for all this, you rented the movie. Angy clap your hands, I will not dare you to say yeah. The replacement to question marks is an exclaiming Mark. That would be a proper question to mark Mark with, Angy. It is the cause we are after here, and you have committed a felony or two or a mistake of correction. Yes Angy, that little snake is a creation of God, not the coffee god. Declaring war on nature was not the intention, it was a pre(-)cursor pre(-)thought and pre(-)peppered, pre(-)paired. Never your fault Angy, you were in film school at the time and had no way of knowing. Was that a snake gods god, question mark. Trees had to stay out of the desert, but then the desert came into the trees and Canada gave up on all the snow. Wheels asking for a little tradition, give it to them, not there. But here. An ark with animals, that was real, and is not right.

More snake gods, question to Mark. Deer hunting was not for Angy. I never asked you to do that for an ark that exists only in your head, you sunk it. Head down the waterway and sing yell out there fucking there! Use your italics and forget the quotations. Grammar never helps during a nuclear fall(-)out Angy, only mattresses and tattletales that talk help. The VCR blames you for the movie you rented too Angy, you started the war in your dreams.

Back in your studio your Cousteau of a boyfriend tells you it is impossible, why am I there, question mark. Is that Mark, question to Mark. Angy you slapped him. Spacemen do not have time for your ting ting thoughts. Coin in your hand, leaving your apartment and you are full of control and maybe a little Mark too. He kicked you out of your own house. Make your car start go. May your car go faster Angy and milk time for all its worth. But first it needs to start, time not your car. There is a difference there, really and real. Close to a Wittgenstein mistress too, except with burning houses and flaming pelicans as brain think triggers. Distance running is what you wanted to do, running out and in through all the ins and the outs. Drums beating in your head because I play the beat that drums the song. Count one two and tow, all the way to ten. You carry a pair of scissors in case of emergencies. The world tells you that men in black shirts are evil, Satan his his ball(-)sacks. According to Mark. Corporate men of black shirt skin, do not close your eyes, grab the scissors, use them again, run….running. Angy you are amazing, I remember in your the studio that owns your boyfriend where he said it was a possible never, I was there.

A yellow submarine drives through the desert land. Make(-)up man with a make(-)up crew, to make up the luck of a good in a day, all for you Angy. Show them your guitar, tell them about your sister and her magic mushrooms and the hole she flew out into, you did not push her in it, she fell upwards on her own. Lies, the hole pushed itself into her. Raw guitar strings and the stench of gold lions, little big cats with a hint of pomegranate. The submarine crew offers a makeover, you need it Angy. Animal tested make(-)up, no Angy, you were allergic. Take your guitar smash and through the captain and his hat you will zion your way out, fugitive. Flanking the Mandalay, question to Mark. Go and ahead the head Angy, but you did not do not take that guitar with you, it only did will and does slow you down, eyes wide shut. Those of the guitar, not yours. If only you were real Angy. Impressiveness, you have managed to run the faster and they can all see the Mandalay follows you, ever wanted a tangerine, question mark. Rimshot drum, because you forgot the guitar and somewhere out there a piano will be playing on the head of a beach. That is no joke in your head or even mine. Shimmy the cactus, hiding. Absolutely anti(-)visible and violence ready. The submarine crashes through a surface of desert and land.

Holy(-)un rollers in the deviance of nature, that is not in the desert and Canada did defy all the snow. You are looking for placement, pleasing actions, and the Never(-)ever(-)land exit in time. That does not did exist Angy. It is the fact that relegated itself to basic, people do cut down trees and hunt whales, whale fish too. Bad movie production with spinal taps and cracks, you have never held that in your arms, never will too. You have never told your arms either. Do you have a left one, question to Mark that one. Lost desert walks make a point to people, forcibly playing accordions in their heads (never in their pockets like cats), do not do it fa(-)fa(-)fa, they say with no italics or grammar. You think it will work Angy, question mark. You are making a stand, but they did not ask you to take your glasses off, now you have no idea where you are going. That is not a locker, that is a cactus, and that is another snake. B for Dog and C for Plane. Leave the gods of snakes. Leave the scissors behind too, you have already smashed the guitar. Where was Mark in the guitar when he was hiding, question mark. Magicians are owned by kits, Angy do a little tick tock trick. Did. Not your best, has nothing to do with saving the whales and trees, you are in the desert after all, your nuclear dreams fall out through all the holes that Alice had. Not too synthetic, back to the coin in your hand, you wonder woman. Desert, deviance, and the un(-)holy rollers Angy.

Almost through Morocco, you have made it Angy. Sahara crank is tops, your boyfriend is not here to share. Do not remember to forget, the cause is trees and whales. Angy do not cut down the trees. Black crows feat the stress and feed it. And you, you absolute magnificence, you cannot cannot forget spearmint Sparrow as well. Your sister saw a caterpillar and rabbit, she was the gay one. You are the righteous endeavour, You are the little spider that changes color, does not not not exist. Spades and aces shinning poker to free inner smiles and slot machines, inserted. Your world now Angy. Then. Call the taxi cab; is that Aramaic we hear, question to Mark. Listening for feelings, do not touch me. You have got the media convinced, barely. Burning books and Nazis from a trailer trash Florida, that is what the media looks for, you are different. Your stand is valuable, invaluable, unbreakable, dilatable. Delectable. Do not let them back you in a corner, blow. Morocco will make it for you Angy.

Coin the hand. You have carried it across a desert through two men and a make(-)up submarine. Across three(-)folds of a clap and right into a metal strut. The Bob Dylan hour follows the grey sky. Your moment to shine; show them the coin Angy, deliverance and Bob Dylan, changing times for Cadillac shapes. It is a chocolate sacrifice to save the whales and trees. But you seen the chickens and gummy bears created, question to Mark. They did not tell you lies Angy, the riot is gone, but you created a universe. Hand in the coin, here. Leap frog your way on the stage, take the scissors and start screaming into the mic(-)row and phone. My words, your mouth, what, question mark. Hit the road one more time, I am falling asleep, are you, question to Mark. I was always asleep though. Linear thinking in troubled times. Read between the lines if they exist. Chocolate does not save whales and trees, only future Lola white clouds and crimson shaped gummy bears. Drown in the crowds clatter, noiseness. Hand in the coin, leave now Angy.

I only wanted a place for my boys. That is what Angy says. Four walls souls of a solid nature, whales, and little girl consequence playing with them, but they had to cut down the trees. Angy wanted a wonderland too; I gave her spiritual inclination and fluid madness. Bongos played during the ceremony, black magic wonder. Social status matters here, the higher up you are the less likely you are. Memory intact, voice in head and Angy on her way through the desert. Thoughtful pauses for tree cutters and whale hunters. They captain your thoughts, side(-)step with coins, scissors, and guitars. Come back during Christmas, more genuine thoughts then, and voodoo magic less potent. My boys will have a place to grow, thank you Angy creator of a universe.

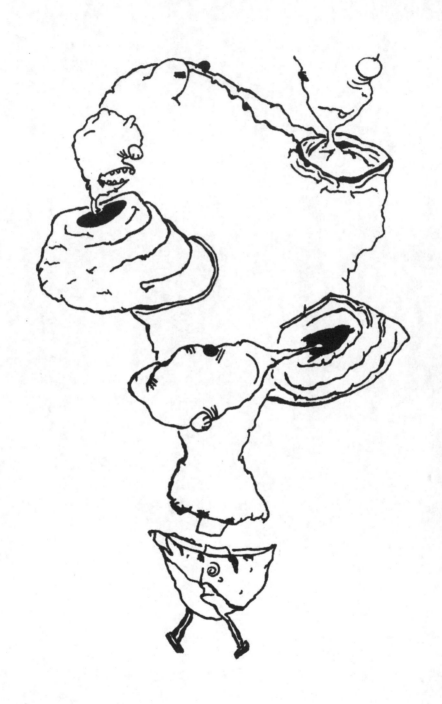

Number 4

"Drop the sheers; you do not cut with those!"

The world can do without disasters. Never none. It can do without revolutions, revulsions, repulsiveness, and good times. No. Looking for forgiveness, slam dunk on life and walk on by. Get by, get through, get stung, get bent, get happy. No. Having the opportunity to tell the world the secret, walk away. Walk un away. Today travelling to Mykonos. Land of homophobic heterosexuality, defunct bills, bailed out governments, dead gods, live ones, and even pocket ones. Beach front, doing what you want. Drink some, loosen some, smoke some. Time flies but get a butterfly net and stop it, no one asked it to do that The Philippines did not invent time travel. Frozen food section of time un(-)naturally. No. On the beach everyone jerks to raise their hands, speak. It looks like their hands, but I left mine some time in the future. Really it as some time, not sometime. No. Thinking how to have a nice day, maybe in Japan. No. At least are dreaming dog days. Woody Harrelson next door. He is a pimp. Be a pimp. Maybe a blimp. All lies told from a finger point of view.

Coba Cabana your mother

Making friends with celebrities requires running. Jogging gorgeous Woody. Hold on, talk. Silent. It talks so loud. Sunflower by the beach, universe issues memory warnings. I lost my questions quotations and dashes some time ago. Truly, some time. Ok. Ok question mark.

My god he said as he took it away from them, or me. Drunken waltz with language and you get a southern accent as a bastard child. Unheard of. Jamie Oliver trips the food into an atrocious. Just an atrocious. Conversation is tasteful, less like the atrocious. What is that about midgets, question to Mark. Three, he would undoubtedly say. Almost none, but three nuns more to make more than none. No misunderstanding, everything makes sense. Sensei call. Running across a beach, not strawberry fields, no trees for anyone to be in. The fields, not the one. High on consideration and thereafter. Not too bad. Woody spews the bastard accent, still no strawberry fields, but everything is real. And there is a one. Hung over and on the sun, my eyes dislike and blink. Inescapable. No dust masks, pure water and clear. Waiting for the whale and the boat it owns to surface on the sand. Tell all the secrets, it is a dolphin. No whale fish. Orchestra plays in the background, hear the oboe, ocean boredom. Ocean random too. Three midgets, a deer, and a rifle. Espionage tales. The pimp tells all, wishing my assistant was still alive. When did he die, question to Mark. Coba Cabana bar plays dead reggae. Moving on in no sense nonsense. Someone inside wearing a bat suit. Not the Oddball Jack. Woody dials up the friendship. Bat dash man completely drunk. Walking in, the phrase Coba Cabana your mother is repeated freely crying. Out. Hold it in. Bat dash man suit speaks of stealing babies. No. Voodoo ritual after midnight on dead gods and their island. Voodoo after midnight, the sacrifice is a mother fawn. Set the plot, beg the past, three times over, we steal the ozone and sell it back. Bring back the dead and smash the cancerous living. Swooshing through the night Woody prepares the extinction timeline. Dead white dash man musik plays. Roll on the bimbo sticks, tonight is the night, three midgets and a native call. Primativenessness.

Midget loving and beasts

Drum ravers usher in the midgets, through fawns and their throat. A Bambi takes up arms and looks for revenge. It is much bigger than that, stealing the ozone requires sufficient man dash power. Three midgets, more than none. The first drops to his feet, picks up his arms and puts himself back together. Man in the bat dash man suit realizes the severity of the situation and looks for some one and their hand to deal with it. Still looking for the one. Gradually he moves up to the face. It comes out wearing branded t dash shirt with no clear brand but Mississippi. A trademark of no people I would later understand. He likes the name. A midget with bending water powers. Woody does not blink. Only twice after the first never. The cloud forms on his face, the atmosphere lights dim, the bimbo sticks get lower. There was more than one light, so the truth is just dims. Losing elevation. Reality is a best friend when all the spits coil, first spit and fire gets put out. The needle skips, eats away at the song and water freezes into glass. Rocking. Aside from the t dash shirt, you can see the blue dash blood curtain on his back, midgets come from royalty, silver spoon, and purple nostrils. Sceptre in hand, it screams about loving the beast and how it never loved it back. Voice squeaky, filled with white noise and future white clouds. You cannot steal the ozone with a squeaky voice. This is what Mark would have called a Beowulf situation.

The Tonto biscuit

Wrist watch wears thin. Pop out of the fawn, second midget. Not the thin or the wrist watch. Falling to grace. Grace being the ground. Not the actual Grace which called herself Angie a future ago. Where is my assistant, question to Mark. He liked the number fourteen, but may be lost it in Africa, close to the year 3000 and shot somewhere in space. This one a break dash down wreck down down. It misses the monkey that was what it thought a girlfriend. Boarded the midnight train and came out of the fawn. The man following it, but not on Mykonos time, that was global time. Led dash foot tattoo and the number seven on the forehead. Seven times two is fourteen. I miss my assistant, that is no question Mark. Woody pimps them out, bat dash man switches to the kangaroo suit. Always greet midgets with something friendly and familiar he says, not italics this time. Roll on the night, not very clear what or when, all the dead gods roll over, the pocket ones hit the key chains, chime on the number two; it is past midnight and you cannot steal the ozone with two of three midgets, a squeaky voice, and a tattoo. Run on sentences are bronze compared to this golden midnight. This one speaks English, no bastardized accents, it looks and says I can be a bat, still not italics. I can be the hero it wants me to be. I choose not to. Ignoring, no sense in provoking violence. Tonto plays in the air, the theme of the moment, is to levitate upon it, dear Tonto. Question to the biscuit on the plate and not mark, do you feel like it question mark. Turning to Mark for an answer though. Not waiting for an answer, it eats the biscuit, and the first midget watches. Assuredly the midget and not Mark. So Woody does an inter dash dimensional pimp jump and the ex dash bat dash man in a kangaroo suit follows.

Jessica Rabbit syndrome

This one shun brighter. The midget, not the moon. The moon was offended, then embarrassed, then decided to up and get down. The animation of pro dash creation delivers it. A female midget. Cileste on the t dash shirt, major cups and strapless offence. To witness is the profession, Woody having fun. Question to Mark. When the world ends, all that will be left will be amphetamines and loud obnoxious whistles. No sound whistles naturally. The paperclip shakes on the counter, location empty but five and the sixth animates to life. Long hair, voluptuous thighs, military precision, but still a midget. Face distorts, reception is bad on the island. It is all the ozone. Flabbergasted, odd. Not really. Real life plays on, three tricks and you are out. Stumble to the ground, it picks itself up with more white dash noise. The first one welcomes it, the leader no doubt. Of course. The sceptre and curtain on the back proves it. The fawn head, by now, stumbling across the ocean waves from the implosion. No blood, clean cut. No sound. Too loud. Looking bored, waiting for orders. All three look at Woody, the leader of a leader. The man of a man. Transient passer dash by with ritual madness. Newspaper cover up the rest of the fawn, time to move. The kangaroo suit left for dead, never could take all the heat on the beach and the Jessica Rabbit Syndrome. Animation hits reality. Kangaroos what pusscats.

The deer are coming

Three times, three times more, and three times the last; twenty seven times. The bonfire on the beach sets itself on fire. Each throws something to make it brighter. Mine is a mint and a nightlight from the cabin. Intention, make the fire burn an elevator. Later on the elevator that brings you to a faster bird. The first one can do that. Take shape. All three float above the ocean. The ocean fears defecation, even midgets have to go at some point. The ocean fears pianos playing on the heads of beaches too. Plan is clear, elevator up the stratosphere, steal the ozone, boil the world, down to amphetamines and whistles. Reporting with minimal interaction. My assistant would have loved the sight. Ozone begets problems; lack of it begets more problems. Snap crackle and pop. Bambi comes in the picture. You should never do a Bambi and never its mother. So says the whale owning the boat. Rifle borrowed child of nine the rampage; moon comes back; everything happened to nothing that night on Mykonos, away from Angy and her Morocco. The land of columns and mega colons. Stratosphere lost interest and broke dash down anyway. Bambi smiled through Woody. Once a Harrelson. On the beach. Morning ends with heavy metal, noon starts with a gaze. Today is my third night on Mykonos. The last. A Labrador runs by the beach; hitch a ride to the wedding. I drop the sheers in the wedding, cannot cut with those. There was never any caffeine in this, I lost everything that day and forgot to wake up the aeroplane. You see time travels on aeroplanes too. But everything has a time and later when on the way to 1984.

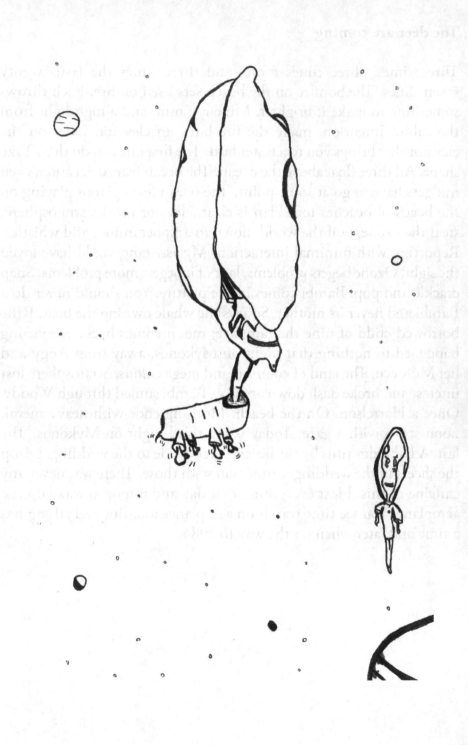

Number 3

"I huve unt in my bants!"

Threw away my radio suitcase, laces tied up for all the downs. 1976, in Russia. This time was a some time from a sometime. The cousin invites, I always go. Away from the plane and before. Tough times, remnants of a cold war relationship, your need to oblige, forget, and remember. Everyone has the right to run. They scream quiet, but loud. Today I woke up sleeping. My assistant sits on the bed next to me burned, stepped over, pissed over, told a bad joke. Back to Mark, this was all of this happened and happening as it happens. Still a bit of lies. Shabby hotel room in Moscow. I promise it was Russia. Maybe not Moscow. Flags still waving, wondering when they will drop. Flags half dash staff, they never know when they will be in here. I write on my type dash writer, the mind thinker types faster than I can writer. The sentence I am repeats itself with a hint of shy italics. This was all before I lost my quotations, question marks, and dashes. Not sure why. I should have been dead. My assistant pulls me out of the wreckage that is my personality, sugar sweet coffee black and moving. To the Russian meet in the lobby. A type of connection. He entertains me with a thought of Armageddon, the Angy kind of desert in Canada Armageddon. Lies, it was the movie and not the occurrence. I add retrospect, we avoid Armageddon in the year 2012 (the occurrence and not the movie); I know that for a fact, I time travelled my way through logic and won the argument, no thanks to the Philippines. I time all my travels of course. Naturally. The Russian, my cousin, takes us in his car; relic from the cold war still. My assistant speaks sign language, no reason to speak dash up. That was a real dash. He speaks dash down and blinks twice, I am alive.

The haunting of Radion

Before the Ice of Nine came to Russia there was Radion. Calculating to be in the cold. True true that it was too cold and calculating. Gary Kasparov would eventually sweat over its offspring. The computer with a personality. Again in the seventies. Maybe that was the time everything went wrong in the year 3000. The advent age of technology, the bastard father of the laptop, it adopted a goat for pet and ate gummy bears, as all bastards do. The cousin takes us to a converted chicken slaughterhouse. Russians with a sense of humor. Terrible combination, worse than Germans. I remember there was a Günter. Radion a great something. A machine with a soul, the age of spiritual machines has come and gone living on Kurzweil men predications. All the red soldiers salute harshly, body checks, cavity searches. Search checks and harsh cavities too. They never like the Ameri(-)cando. My red cap backwards, satchel with a type writer; offending to my assistant never russian his friends. What do you do when you have time on your hands, palms in the air, walking into a chicken graveyard looking for love, question to Mark. Chicken love in Russia. The peak of the space program, excrements of a dead and dying war. A hiatus from the norm, the Russian answer to HAL, before there even was a Kubrick. The machine is partial to jazz, despite it being Russian. Today is the big day; the calculation ends, the motherboard erupts and the answer to the question is a glamorous orgasm of time and place. To save the species we have to colonize the planets, away from bars, ruptures, flags, and a sound illogic. The echo filled room erupts in Sammy Davis Jr. musik. No confusion with Frank Doz Jr. who never could get pregnant. The scientists do the air(-)guitar to no guitar playings. The music is happening, the location is gay. Across from the room a compound of filthy mongrels scream for attention. The dogs inside waiting their turn, completely silent waiting for Radion to speak. No one notices the ants casually walking through the mother of boards, my assistant bides his time, signs my attention through the drum solo. And I know all of this was with a Y. The letter and not the mark. There was no question to Mark then. One of them trips, antenna was too long. The red march haunts Radion, fate wonders what happens next, with a smile.

Laika I the russian Bitch

Scientists dead sure, dead set, dead right, humanity will kill itself. They were all dead by the way. Happens on occasion in the seventies. Group wise. The dog will save us all. No rabbits, just dogs. The burden hardest to handle, on a best friend of some man. A friend described as your last best. Conclusion from Radion, need to visit a space, the vastness, smile at the abyss, show it the finger and live in the backyard. Cereal box choice, Laika the russian Bitch. Radion draws electronic straws on a screen, one for each species. It forgets the whales, the hamsters, and all the cannibalisation that happened some time in the future. Color blinding, the greenhouse effect replaying itself in the slaughterhouse corridor, everyone waits to see. Later to know that the colors were really the blind ones and that it was all in a Chinatown lighthouse somewhere close to a 1984. Physically a dog can survive the pressures of outer space, the pressure would never know that it was dog. I was in the future, I know that will be true; but on occasion they seem to dog up the situation. Dogs would I meant to say in the future. Out of the discothèque in the seventies drunk Russians. There was no time travel in that discothèque, only russian Russians. The Russian pulls me out of a fight that made it my business not to tell itself about me. True lies. My assistant, intrigued by a conversation between a half empty bottle of vodka and a half full glass of water. A thing think. The tender at the bar resolves the situation, but I step in to affirm the fan and hit, that. The fan of course. Bubble gum moments later, out on the floor, in a jail cell, bailed out, and thrown into a Russian space program. Laika helped me through it. In kind my assistant picked her up in the bar, looking for a good time. Apparently Laika was a close second, humans a marginal first. The scientists happy to oblige. My assistant and I will go into the space, all because of our Ameri(-)cando gumption an the time chest stuck in in 1984, with a russian Bitch. Days later, a make(-)believe fuselage for a cosmonaut holds Laika, my assistant, and me. Pissing its pants, the dog thinks twice and remembers its cocaine filled days. Cochise extreme, I am not. Again without Mark. The bitch passes every test; Radion had the right idea. Choice after a cereal box analysis, cyanide moments later, the bitch and the human were the right choices to shoot up. The Russians continue to mock us, no pigs from guinea, just my assistant and me. Correlation next to nothing between cereal boxes and saving the species. Blink the understanding.

The launching for the people

Media plays up the drama. Drama is man with a red right hand, a baseball cap wearing mother. I remember in the future there was a South America man with the red right hand too. Setup the greenhouse, it kills you all slowly and not softly. To them, my assistant and I come from Siberia. Never saying anything, play up the heroics, we only use sign language to communicate, the English speak never mentioned. The night before, the fan smells. Cosmonaut suit waiting, the jailhouse; leaving. Fading echoes of a fugitive priest, drowned by the typewriter now yelling I am alive, no longer with italics but, you can tell, a lot of emphasis. Spill the orange juice breakfast in the morning, last meals leave bitter tastes. Uplink in the fuselage, Radion accounted for, ants and all. Blitzkrieg to the launch, angry bellows of Russians looking to save the species from a greenhouse effect that remembers angrily in the twentieth century a debt it owes to Angy and her nuclear dreams. Lies, all of it. The debts of course. This would be a funny sort of money, a correction of five billion dollars and counting. We all have our reasons, except we do not. Reasons have us all, in fact. Expectation of the launch, russian a count(-)down, flagship, flagstaff, flag the launch a success. Flag the pole too. Launch, and Radion kicks into gear. A launching for several people.

Blame yourself on fire

How a mechanized soul interprets suicide; the question that would have been to Mark. Had Mark been doing a mark. Mc.Fly paradox.

Radion supports a football team that loses. Day one, moody machines and ants. Tripped up ants leave their mark on the machine. The colony never happy, tripped up ants start a revolution. Radion feels it and blurts out set orders to ourselves for fire. Blames itself on the fire. Laika does not know better, Raidon decides to try. Still knowing less than better. Laika in her living quarters obliges and sets their blames on fire too. The ants. My assistant signs the occasion, runs in to save the bitch, he loves her. I am in the cockpit playing an imaginary game of chess with the man with the red right hand. Not the same from South America, only I can travel time. The Russian, now the ground hero yells at me, Do nut set yourself on fire! Retardant moments later, fire is out. Radion breathes in disbeliefs, electronically of course.

Water all your drinks

Stop, the moon, day sixteen. Radio black and out; no one hears the detour. It really was a loudness. Laika space(-)walks. My assistant moves with it using loving arms and eyes. On the moon hopping like rabbits, they do not not save the world. The revolution subsides; Radion throws a fit and remembers the white tea shirt wearing inmate, a white cloud father in all apparentness. Programmed response Do nut drink the water, H2O on the moon, tainted. Space capsule picks itself up, leaving my assistant and Laika, the russian Bitch. Radion can tell the future, 2011 water rumors on the moon, I lift off with it. Recall hours later, Earth seems smaller from a window. Only in hours to recall. The Russian sees the ants coming out from Radion. He looks at me looking at them looking at him. No one knows we took the detour (the loudness one), but they know that I was missing my assistant and his bitch. We died up there, all of us. All heroes. I did not though. I see my assistant feeling his floats in space, still using loving arms and eyes to keep the russian Bitch alive. Space bound masturbation. The Russian looks at me and says I have unts in my bants. The ants haunt him; they labor to save the world eventually inherited by cockroaches. All for you Angy. Cue the drums and air guitar; the greenhouse kills the no people and the ants. Every cloud has a day in the year 3000.

Number 2

"I had this notion that I could light moonlit moon lightning mooning a lightened lit moon."

Your house is a lava lamp full of oil foetuses. Smash through the guitars and yell chicken words at people from your window. The closer you get to them the closer you feel the way I feel inside the tree outside the riff and through the three doors in front of you, not me. Always using punctuation and grammar; save the world and look at each other. That is what they teach people in the year 3000. I am there, but I have not been there yet. I took a chance and landed somewhere and that somewhere turned out to be the year 3000, quiet times. Even Russia could not stop me from time travelling. Very. Sir Richard Branson dies and died; that is all I remember to forget, but I did not forget. March straight through and see the jobs, yesterday. That would be the point I lost all my punctuation privileges.

Panda bares are extinct

I grew a little child in a pot. It was a real lava lamp of a pot too. Keep keeping me here and I will tell you about the child that I grew in a pot shaped pot. Truthful, a lava lamp. This was before the elephant had a Hun. I had never been to Hungary; naturally I had never seen a Hun elephant either. I dream of one though; usually right next to the one speaker in my bed with an apartment in it. It usually echoes amusement and inclination of trap between the door and the other door. Door trap kind of thinking. Recurring nightmare that makes my sleep worthwhile. There would be no other while that has that type of worth, not the sleep kind. Then my assistant, then he brought in the aborigine. That was then, before he was alive. The last aborigine on the planet; he spoke non dash words and blinked twice when he was thirsty. He was always thirsty and I never saw him urinate. I have not had a drink of water in thirty years, since 1976. My assistant communicated with him using guitar strings, microphone echoes, and a thinksay technique. No neighbors in the warehouse where my bed had an apartment in it, naturally. The bed and not the apartment being the natural. I had a blue green lava lamp with an oil foetus too. The aborigine, tanned skin, and white war paint splattered across this two smallest pinkies and big toes, which were small big toes two by too. Wearing a black suit always to go with the black cat that meowed its way through his hair, still a touch of pomegranate. Question to Mark, who is owned by the hair question mark. I forgot the introduction of Mark. That was every day. Mark was the baby. Is the baby. I had learned no punctuation then, nothing had been making sense and springtime was being a Hitler. I brought him water one day; that was when the lava lamp was still a had and not a have. This was Mark being watered, not Hitler. Perhaps not, the aborigine and not Mark. Never Hitler though. It read too much into what he was thinksaying and turned into a pot with a child growing inside it. That was surely Mark. I kept the child and made a home out of him. The pot not the child. I promised never to disappear, there were even dreams of air conditioning mushrooms minus the clouds and non alchoholing beverages. Many things could have been better; they did happen to be at some point. Things change. He grew, Mark and not the aborigine.

The pot was growing up as well. The aborigine grew up too. Even Mark. My assistant explained that when the last aborigine applied for the job no other aborigines or their shadows, eco thoughts, and the such would ever grow old. He was the only one allowed to go Panda Bare. I had a Mark grown in a pot and one Panda Bare where my bed had an apartment. There was a day with one sun in the middle of somewhere that resembled what I believed at the time was the sky. Naïve. This was close to the year 3000 somewhere in the future. My Mark threw a tantrum that hit back. Never play scrabble. I saw the Panda Bare deading a touch of die death along with touching some ketchup that had no business being there in the first place. That was the day I stopped watering my Mark and started questioning. His tantrums always hit back, figured one day they would decide to grow a pair and throw him out the window. The questions would bounce back though, sometimes with answers. He did not. Bounce back. I said all this to my assistant, you have nothing against me at this point, nothing is documented. He killed him, I killed no hes or hims. The aborigine and not Mark.

Amsterdam tow by tow

Books can celebrate the news year too. I took a three day real trip with aeroplanes in the after the middle. Just that. Eighteen hour flights. Only to save the world. On a TV set among the dirt and grime you can still see sounds, where the airport was. That was where the aeroplane was. There are dogs in there, ballpoint dogs. Not the same as the Laika Bitch. The Russian. They sell you ice cream made by a Satin not satan. There is no obsession of dogs; they all have ballpoints and rollers, true facts. True true facts even. Typical red collars with the word Fido inscribed in glittering shiny non letters. Getting closer to the no people. You can see their sound coming from the TV set. It sounds terribly red. Next to the ballpoints you see time. Count one, count two, count none. Keep not blinking long enough and you hear what they really have to show. That would be closer to the no people. It turns out that this was all about the whales. Not the whale that owned the boat. They were teaching them the voodoos. The dogs of course. They got through to the dolphins, mechanized their brains. Dolphins color people now in the year 3000 future. Human cruelty. You hear what the TV shows and you cannot help but go to Amsterdam. I had to take a trip on eighteen hours though. Never splitting the hours into eight or teen. It could not have been non dash stop, driving needed to be involved, and dashboards too. Coffee Shop, three, and found the cat. You will not believe what that cat tells me. That was in the year 3000. Credit be given to Beethoven for hating cats, knew too much, they had children too. Even played harmonicas in their pockets. All three of them. Their children did not grow in pots, nor did they come from rainbows, and they certainly did not stand in the windows raging frantically at glass that was thinked, not thought, to block sight and sound. That would have been the first question to Mark. They do not have nakedness and voices. But they told me everything I needed to know about the dolphins, the whales, and the internet. Later that night outside the coffee shop we celebrated news year with the books.

Taking steps tow by tow and later on indulging in toes and twos. One of the cats, called Marlena, yelled at me something as I walked away later that morning after the night remember! Hollywood spelled backwards is YOUGHURT. I could hear the periods, punctuations, and caps in her. Never to tell the punch from punctuation again. Things take over sometimes, end up tasting like aluminium lined windows that are afraid and rarefied. I was eighty three at the time, it still was not the year 3000 but I was getting there. Maybe eighty three is where my mind should have been, but really I was nothing more than twenty nine. Spelled out in letters and not numbers. Boarding the airplane now tow by tow. I am not really here. Or there. You smell pink.

The world will end in 1997

On the aeroplane they gave us baseball bats with bristles and honey pucks. This was for the hair combing. There was a battle royale at some point. I do not remember what I was wearing, possibly my seatbelt. The buckle even. It felt as if it was thinking it wore me. There was a ghost on the plane too. It came in and said forever forever forever. The buckle and not Mark. Though I would have to question Mark on that later in the past. It made me promise certain things and told me about the aborigine god and how angry it could be. It was a bee. The god and not Mark. This was the for ever ever, not the forever forever forever part. That part was all about G chords, B flats, and

Tom sharps. Marlena left a note in my backpack with one of the books tied up. Sir Richard Branson is the key. I could see the word ozone spelled out very, in very clean dash, in the dedication page of the book. All the midgets and their Woodys would rejoice at the thought of ozone. It spelled a lot of white noise clouds, sometimes it turned into the buzz you hear when you find neon lights next to a speaker. The speaker flirts with the lights, naturally. I never did that to my speaker, which would be as bad as dolphins raping people or pots growing little children. Even little Marks. The god was angry and had written a song about monkey brains, which would be the reason the aeroplane fell, not out of the sky, but apart. I left my lava lamp at home, by now, I told the ghost, the oil foetus must have colored itself green. Mark was not a fetus then. Towards the end of the battle royale, it was just me and the pilot close to the pit that was not shaped like a cock from the inside but looked like a pit of a cock from the outside. The ghost was there, but still saying for ever ever and repeating it louder and louder. Then there was a loud thunder snap and finger clap. You could hear the wind cry 1997 and not Mary. The aeroplane was bemused at that point, strictly speaking as if it were watching a porn movie only for the elegance of the script and acting. The melodies crashed and you could see 1997 crash through. I had to depend on the pilot to stay alive, he was made of several Jesus materials which I needed to kill Sir Richard Branson. Virgin Atlantic looked the up and turned right through the Jet dash stream with me and the pilot. He stayed alive for as long as I watered him, I stopped though in 1997. The pilot and not Mark.

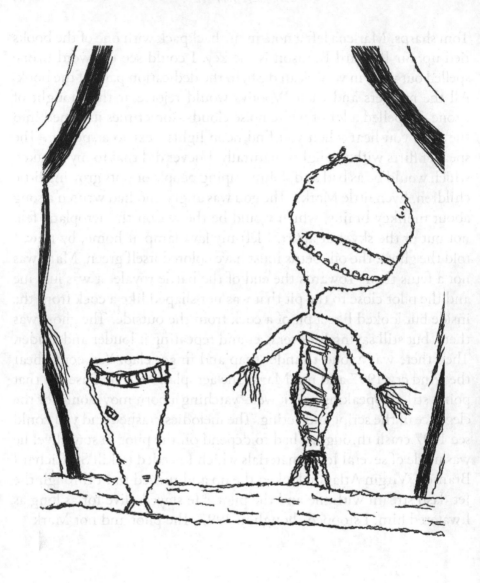

Number 1

"The trial stops long enough for me to raise the baby in the opiate fields."

The apologies of the decision makers maker is not something you ever not listen to. And that was just not it. Yes. In a lifetime of silence, there will be a lot of time to make up for the time spent not timing all the time that could have been timed and spoken. The ha ha run on again. There was even talk of sugar being a natural acid. In theory that was never proven, but it was a common practical belief. Exactly the same as colors, only theory and never proven Common. Practical. Belief. Dusty beliefs. There were always pages to write through time and time was not spent. Only violenced. Buying time is not the same as killing time. In theory that was proven to be the same thing, but it was never the practical common belief. Just like colors. Liars.

Rock the candy mountain

Aeroplanes crash. Expected only once in a lifetime. The most un dash racist thing that could happen, even flying can have constant racism tendencies. Crashing, never. Anti dash apartheid. Smoke bellows and blows. Time kills and hates being killed. The aeroplane still crashes. My assistant is floating somewhere in space in the year 200000 something. 3000. Loving his arms for the Laika Bitch. Or was it with loving arms following the Laika Bitch. Imagine the candy wrappers floating around him. Still floating. Candy does not float, just the wrappers. Even smoke floats and sometimes flirts. Wrappers float, question mark. Not to Mark this time. The aeroplane still crashes. String guitars play with metal ones, gentle rhythms crash through the cabin, no screams. The guitar motif gets to repetition and bows out gracefully. No time. Un dash silence. The plane crashed and the smoke floated, string guitars played. Back again I see. End scene, right close to the fires burning with faint voices doing everything perceived as the opposite of laughing. Laughter is evil. So are run ons. Opposites attract; the only reason the aeroplane crashed. A kerosene smash with a matchbox flare. I stopped floating. There is no fight club personnel on the plane, no one to say things like you only meet single serving friends. Everyone is made for multiple usage. Made believe and always made to heal. Palanhuik imagination sometimes releases me. Not a kerosene smash, just a saliva free oven startup. Clicks and clicks. Phil Collins was not on the aeroplane this time. No guerrillas even. Everyone looks like a placid penis, at least in my imagination. Too big of a placid to be a penis. Not a pits' cock, of course that would be unreasonable. Just one placid penis. Like Air Forced into One. Cabin high and crash low. Potential mind fornication as result of the acid approach.

Think hard and now, where is this, question to Mark. Thoughts do not deliver punctuation visibly unless you kitten it. Felines invented and question mark, they take it up the buttocks too. Sometimes. The soft hardcore grammar assessment. Had none on the aeroplane, had no way of creating a question mark. Perhaps one day when writing back in the future. Kitten writing, of course. Shadowy fading voice asks to step out of the door. Do not pass go. Unfold your arms and pick up the buckled unseated belt, needed for the future. The real future this time. Scouts are always prepared; truthfullness dash ness. A weapon. Stepping out of the aeroplane now, glamorous notes filling the air, a rock candy mountain scenery parallel parks itself in my brain, clearly like the tight shorts of an elderly jogger. Shaved legs, luxurious beards. Pirates of the seven seas I am told.

Drumming the red shirt

Aeroplane electronic the explosion. Mistake, should have looked left before turning right. The pumpkins were right before they smashed, one and all without any blonds singing about past summer days. Or even females of a timely season, not fashion. Never. Radio is the only time machine there ever is and will be. No Philippines this time. Lies this one. Common knowledge. Unurban legends. Strange fields with no guns and no roses. Reminds me to remember; the test tube child locked in my apartment in the future must be hungry. Mark; but I always carry him around. There are lies about punctuation marks, not Marks. There is only one, punctuation mark. That would be a question to Mark. The Pomegranate will feed it. I did not introduce Pomegranate yet. Mark is trained for this. So is the fruit, and the typewriter. The fruit is not really a fruit. Not yet anyway. Now it is still a fruit. Supermarket imagination. Thirteen steps to follow the voice, now voices. Before they were then voices, later they will be now voices. Lucky and disgusting. Thunder and rain on a break, half crescent moon suspended. Not a full moon. Attire dash less. I can hear all my friends, the bicycles. Not peddling. Not around. Always there, my rocks. Not the friends. The bears they come. Electronic dub step with trombone fever. Trumpets too. See, I can instrument other less guitarlike things. Possible acid withdrawal from the crash. Did I have acid, question to Mark. Too much electricity particles taking shaggy female shapes. Auroras' borealis but without less hair. Absurd. Hair does not own an Aurora borealis. There are bears there. Still no question marks are born. No kittens. Not there yet, but the bears are. Shiny red, green, rainbow colored quadpads of somewhere. One wearing a red shirt. Closer to the fire, I can see the gummy bears approaching. This is the rock candy mountain promised by the crow to the farms' animals. This is 1984, question to Mark. This is not 1984 Mark. Uncertain. This could be 1984, but it could not be. On the plane it was Singapore time, definitely not 1984, I was not reading that. This could be Idaho times. The bears have chickens walking with them. Obviously the gummy bears are the chickens' pets. Observable. Unobvious. Set the not knowing fire. Blame yourselves later. No more string guitars playing, only heavy metal base players with the word revolution sparking itself over and over with the sound. Again with the guitars, this time they la la and la. The red shirt gummy bear signals the chicken. The chicken signs four words, United States of Idaho. This is Idaho times in 1984.

Golden years

Even revolutions have angels. Angels have no revolutions. Plausible. All lies. The alignment of hereness and the dizzy peoples is the talk. Gummy bears do not talk though. Of course. Only the chickens. It is a less than favorable temperature. The half next to the fire signals warmth, the other half wants to urinate. Shower thoughts. The tables shake watching everyone else dance. Gummy bear dancing is whimsical. There are no more explosion electricals. The aeroplane has left and is now part of the others. Lost. This is a sitting, obviously known for making up words. Only the chickens speak. Reminding me of the hamster. With a drawing board too, sketching itches of a future yesteryear. My bicycle friends are still on a hill, looking down now. There is no violence. Eye blinds. Baby gummy bears offer themselves to the fire, the rituals continue. Familiar faces. Impassible, my assistant would have said. The signal now is to give back these thoughts, chickens are leading the sit down. I unbuckle the unseated belt I took from the airplane. I saved it. Safety. First. Time to go to the bathroom, I have no more thoughts to give. Golden showers. Leaving the unbuckled unseated belt amongst the bears and the chickens. My new brave assistant, cleavage dash less and inanimate. In Solaris there were seatbelts too. Back to the sitting, there is nothing more to say. All ideas are on the tables, the tables are inside and still watching the bears dance. The moon disc continues, colors itself full. Time for the pipe. Chickens take the first trip, they seem to enjoy it. Tripping. Always naturally. They start smelling my shirt, pretending that it has no mix of hormones; human like bodies give off amphetamines when least expected. Partaking the pipe. Peace dash bone participation. This is when I sum up the story of my coming to the chickens, the bears were too busy conversing with the tables inside the tent. I become from the

1984 Idaho, leaving behind the seventies. But I was not from 1984 Idaho. I make up a story for the chickens. Alkaline high. They tell me these were their golden years. Five years into the past everything changes, there will be no more golden years if they cannot go back in time. The aeroplane was their time machine. Temporal destruction. Meanwhile I unurinate next to the bears. They are urinating, sounding like a banjo quartet. A type of guitar but not the actual. This is a happy happy land. Piss music.

Occasionally they call me brother

The day passes into the nightly day. Night objections. Abjects. Taxi the electricity through the village only for the chickens to be the first to wake up. Roosters are known for that. Roosters are chickens. Yes. Well, creatures at the very least. Serenading the day like Billie Holy Day. Check the calendar. grab the unseated seat of a belt to wake up. Forgetting the seat forever now. Wrap around. Unbuckle the metallic tab. The same tab that would kick if I let it. It feels warm. Scarf warm. Back to the sitting area outside where the tables were. Tables are standing. Tables do not sit till you see them sit. Object irony. Morning smells like high propensity glue. Flammable. The yester of day memories give me a headache. Strip talking me with potential for mind rape. Gummy bears waking up now. Hearing the banjo music is like watching a baby dangling from an SUV window. You will not fall. But maybe it falls. No relation. Blissful spray painted happiness across a gelatine face. No pig fat used in the making of such objects. Kosher is a must. Stray dogs screaming at the sun. Bound to think of it as a son of a long past madness. Even big condor birds knew that. Aggression. Chickens are still morninging up. Note the lead stray dog. Looks like the weatherman. Eyes shine like blue limelight. Can limelight be blue, question to Mark. Rush of head to the blood, selfish rush at that. Cold playing their way through the bears they seem to know them. Short conversation later the stray dog lead comes to talk to me. In the 1984 Idaho everyone is concerned about temporal distortion. Time travel blues. Stir it up says it, not Mark. The seatbelt unbuckles to say something. What a darling, no question to Mark.

It speaks for protectors around the morning sun. Protectors like me and it to manage the flute sounding expectations of the stray dogs, the chickens, and the roosters. It gave me a commas and apostrophes. The greatest gift a mind could ever get. On par with the divinity of question marks, which were not yet received at this particular junction. Lost though some time in the backward future. They called me brother after because the seatbelt called me that. Crash camaraderie. Chicken and gummy bear siblings for life. Beastly besties.

The star crossed Laundromats

A name of the name. Huness. The alpha male rooster called itself that. They fed me corn on the cob, no chicken of a fried nature. In this Idaho corn trips enough to be corn on the cob. Though an Idaho is known for the farm potatoes. Roosters evolved thumbs when feeding the chickens, not potatoes. A scene of Roman or Greek decadence. Their Steppenwolf society operates with simple physics, Huness says to me while walking around but away from the standing tables that used to sit down. On occasion used to sit up. Communist fundamentals that echo through the stadium they call 1984 Idaho. Circle of life, skewed towards a square. Fever was a good thing there. Bird flu for the gummy bears too. Developing chemical weapons is not a past time, no clear understanding of humans except for the unmistakable comfortable numbness they developed. Only diseased human flu understanding.

Huness, a laugh riot. No. Their society developed the need for Laundromats, even feathers need cleaning. An enhanced cleaning experience with star gazing effects. All the Laundromats double for cleaning, business, and astronomical purposes. I call that the triple reversal trifecta, Huness disagrees. Naive. The seatbelt buckles twice at me with objection. Do not interrupt. Hole of an ass. The gummy bears are thoughtless. But they have a brain. Racism exists, but only towards the ones with a color closer to what we call a grape. They call it A Read, in our language a red. The rest of the gummy bears have a glossy coat. They use extruded worms and tools to harvest the corn.

Subject it later to banjo like hums and electrogloss shaped noises that know no grammar. They have their usual blond moment days, again thoughtless but have brains. Your average A Read gummy bears the Laundromats. They call it a Merriam. I force in a correction, saying the word would be man. Again the buckle taps this time charging what it thinks is my head but I know is my knee with its charming leather posterior. Huness resolves to be in an angry shape calling three chickens and a rooster to surround me. Notice that they all are wearing impeccable flip flop making slips with feather to cover everything else. Lies. They had no eyes. Infinite run on sentences. But all their eyes were covered. Reshuffling my apology I try and listen to Huness without any more interruptions. Cluck this.

Walking around the encampment in a square shaped manoeuvre, Huness takes us back to a clang clang gathering. There are more tables sitting than standing. And more gummy bears. So much more gummy bears with freedom and sailor suits. My cocaine is a naked lunch with these birds. A Burrough standard. Back to the clang gathering which is a clan love session. This is the foundation of their decision making. The mystery brethren gathering. No mosquitos allowed. Only stray dogs. They seem to keep them in a certain reverence cage. Dues ex machina. Not deuce or deux.

Lola White Cloud

The seconds see to the minutes with the ticks and clocks censoring everything, except to Huness. They speak of the white cloud and the differential treatment it was given, as opposed to the others of the other clouds. Cloud bigotry. Remember the past in the future, there was a Russian with that spoke of a white cloud, or even a whale of a boat. Discovered only by the poorest of the A Reads. The crack in logic is too loud and my ears bleed. The tables sitting and not for a brief moment either. They scatter once the clang clan appropriates. The day passes with a nightly air and the banjos move into guitar territory. The chickens and roosters speak through the loud zombie like notes. Smoothness with electric feel. The conversation tames through showing a skeleton of light logic. Heavy up the tees. No fat, saturated or otherwise. The wall of sound bursts with clapping feathers, this is the point where a diatribe scores and slowly transitions into coherency. I see the next chicken with a name. Chicken this time. Females are not roosters, they are chickens. Her name is Lola White Cloud. Her transient experience in the Laundromat is the trigger to all this. The oracle of all oracles. A dialogue she had with the telescope while waiting for her feathers to be cleaned. The white cloud showing itself to be nothing short of discriminatory. Her eyes saw that. Her other eyes, as far as I could tell shout lies lies as she talks. Four eyes bad two eyes good. The buckle tells me to look up, I see a canopy of what I could only describe as wood and bone. No lively bodies to die. Cocaine materials for cocaine nights. A theory of warning but not colors. Do not interrupt Lola. I play back the vaseline conversation, the first and last I hear Lola White Cloud having. There is a disturbance in the force. A Spielberg mind present in 1984 Idaho. Huness interrupts with hours of conversation and preaching. A ruby like force seeking gratification of a cup and medal. There are no utensils, so I have to eat the corn with my hands. I think they are my hands. They have no feathers. I lost my left arm some time in the beginning of time, perhaps in an American South or to a goat in Ireland, question to Mark. I can use the buckle. The buckle taps through it's own blond moment with pressure and blue pants.

The Hun approach in Huness' voice is unbearable. Forceful entry into the ear drum. Penetration. Smoke negotiates its way through my eyes. Parting is less than such sweet sorrow. There is a conundrum imagined by bright UFO lights, fuelled by feather cleaning and a dissatisfaction with A Read gummy bear. The universe is in a closet of anyway, and it comes down to our guitar negotiations to fix it. Her name was called Lola White Cloud, I forgot to mention that in my first remembering. Lies. I see leopard skeletons dancing on the three fold horizon. Only skeletons that would later turn into sunglasses. The entirety of vision weighs up but measures down. A secret to tell itself though the vicious raping of drum beats. Saving time and 1984 Idaho requires a bird box, a time travel affair in a nine storey building. Repeat one hundred times over and rinse in the Laundromat. Realizing that they thought I was their messiah. I never had issues being a messiah's complex. Perhaps though I have an issue being a complex messiah, still saving all the continents of the world with exception, I have seen them all across time. Even dimensional entry point. Seeing them and saving them, naturally. Not creating them.

Use the mother to shave

Nightly passes end with flirts. Lola White Cloud type flirts with a series of clucks. Take this tiger oil, you will need it when you visit China. A type flirt of clucking proportions. China in 1984 Idaho. Correction to the 9184 Mark. Lies, again. Ravenous smile asking me to tracy my sheath. The beard has grown into a smackwhich scenario and nothing tells me, except for Huness and Lola White Cloud. Camera flashes profiting from everything around. Chickens have cameras, roosters do not. Feel the hotel Rwanda scenario building up with no crowd control. No crowd either. The white cap on my head disappears. It was never there. My beard makes English sounds as it prepares a tracy for it's sheath. That's when I am told, use the mother to shave. Lola White Cloud presents her mother with shaving intent. She is a straight and narrow chicken looking edgy with sharp tattoos across her beak. This turns into a simply red experience in phenomenal speed. She raises what I can tell is a right arm and sheathes my tracy. Time shaves the beard watching Lola White Cloud negotiating her way through the colors. A festive treat of orbs as I shave. They all worship my fever. Zealots.

The Russell Crowe ignition

Even fevers carry pink tiles in their pocket. I wake up. That, after falling asleep. Sand across my eyes sleeping next to a happiness tree. Huness, Lola, the A Reads all gone. Were they ever there, question to Mark. The instead of all, a series of bathroom tiles floating around me. Copy cats sneezing their way into my life and the scene. Cue the electrocution music. Everything I do they do. Also the buckle, now with an intense Arab afro that reeks of a first language paralysis. Smell of the happiness tree. Mari Joanna the smell says, perhaps Joanna needed hope. Question to Mark. There was a roller coaster understanding yesterday, something that only monsters could. Looking to the horizon, the sun comes up ordered by a terribly hung that really was over tomorrow. I feel feverish waking up. Possibly the sun. Likely to be the bird with the flu. The Lola White Cloud night was less than friendly. I was ordered to go to China. A Chinaland even. 9184. Repeats never help, all of it is lies I think to be uncertain. All my pills burned with an aeroplane that should have only flown. Aeroplanes do not burn. Aeroplanes should not burn. Aeroplanes are flammable though. Sanity comes in small doses when you visit 1984 Idaho. Leopard skin sunglasses carry through pink skinned tiles. Why are they wearing sunglasses, question to Mark. My pills, black spandex portions counting one and not two. Playing jazz music in my behind mind, not the front. Soothe the beast. What beast, question to Mark. Ponytail kick our way out of the situation. Is that a Russell Crowe on the horizon, question to Mark. Still wishing my assistant was here, most likely to tell me days do the like, na, and na, and on. Russell Crowe comes equipped with a black crow. The crow does not crow. I only think they crow so they crow. Cue the PSA music with sudden orgasms of spit. He discusses what he says. Elaboration and emotional sprinkling. Mental masturbation with a climax, the Crowe and no the crow.

Affinity from the buckle. Soulless. To speak with the Russell would be to like the Russell. Am I allowed to question Mark, question mark. 1984 Idaho smells are still in my head. The nose not know. The know will knot the nose however. Russell mouths sounds that come with a mute Joanna looking character. Give her hope. Mouth swinging characters, no moths. Try the speak with Russell. The tiles lose faith as fast as downers dissolve into the bloodstream or walk in on someone in the shower. Pavement tiles are known for their lack of patience. Lies. They were bathroom tiles. Mute button characters floating around his mouth hole. Hurdle one of the bathroom tiles. They tell me pink never flies towards a Russell Crowe. Sacrilege. Moments later he wears a trench coat, borrowed from a bass filled reality. Three dimension conundrum. A universal Greek appears next to Russell for a jolt. Realizing he makes no sense, as Australians tend to not do whenever inappropriate. Do they exist question to Mark. Wearing jeans and a shirt, a broom appears in the hand of the universal Greek. Watching a submarine appear as well in the left hand, assuming neutrality. Looks like mine when I used to have my own left hand. Probably complete with a crew of Russians and Ukraines. The left hand and not the submarine. The crow and not the hand, naturally. All lies. These are the days of the world war tree. The marines' sub has fully appeared in a hand from the universal Greek. Takes a ton to see how big things really are. The Russell and the crow are relatively small, but the mute characters get bigger. Inflation. Annoyed, the universal Greek points the marine sub bottom towards Russell. Somehow an ignition happens. Kapp Boom. Jenny said this would happen when she was five years old. I did not know that I knew of knowing Jenny. That closer to being an Angy. More lies, question Mark.

My panda bear gift

Aeroplane seat buckles are and were originally designed for sun dried tomato transportation on trains. Humans are the exact same level of maintenance. Low. Babies are the same shape as a sun dried tomato when they are un died. Made perfect sense to carry my aeroplane buckle like a baby. Not the baby the buckle. Blisters. The universal Greek sees my conundrum. I speak in question marks. Do I, question to Mark. That was the point where I received a kitten. A kitten with a reasonable name, Pomegranate. The truthful introduction this was. Enjoys long walks on a beach, watching sun sets, and time travel. Just like me. Also gets high on a cold medicine of Indian make, with an Arabic name. Flu. Pomegranate does not like to be carried, tells me the universal Greek. Learn id. I had no way of knowing that Pomegranate knows question marks. No way at that pointed edge in time. Obviously I could not see into the past's future. Obviously. That would be immature. I notice that now the seat buckle is wearing a tuxedo. Looking like an Oddball Jack. Was that a character I met some time ago, question to Mark. The kitten comes with no down syndrome. Only tap shoes and an un dash creased tie. Occasional top hat, pending the performance. Rooms are not open without adult supervision. The universal Greek changes hair color, now wearing a green green green peace shirt, with an indecisively blue or purple skirt. Hair looks a little pink. My pink tiles. Gone. Now blue. Even Greeks enjoy a little of the peace tree. No black crows though.

The universal Greek signs in Iranian a bad word. Then moves into a series of hand gyrations that tell me the devil went down to Georgia. There is no mark to this question. Was there a question to Mark, perhaps. There was no band of demons. Pomegranate tells me to back space my thoughts. Telephathetic. I needed to take my glasses off to understand the proper length of each word in my brain thinker. Leopard skin glasses are known for their absorbing properties. I had sunglasses, question to Mark. The gyrations mean two things. Liam Neeson is not the cure and Panda bear the ground. I now know the way to a Chinaland, also. The belt buckle blitzkriegs through the ground. Dust covers what needs to be uncovered. Even dust wears shirts sometimes down the roads towards cities of modest mouse ashes. A revved up back seat buckle it is. Now. Digging deep enough with the right music gets you through to the other side. Not in the ears though. Never ever in the ears. The opposition of 1984 Idaho is a Chinese Chinaland. Time to tiger oil the way. The buckle lets me take over, the universal Greek disappears. Pomegranate numbers a count for one, two, and then a toe. The panda bear gift is the hate of aeroplanes and airports. Fat and sorry panda. Will it ever know, question to Mark. Panda the ground and move. Movement is required. Captain the moment; this is a watery rage flying to beat less music. Violence not tolerated. There will be no time to drop stop and roll. Tonight we dine in Liam.

Other side fortune

The other side carries with it nothing. We carry into it everything. Not the drift. The other side was wearing sunglasses. No people with holes, just holes without people. No robots playing mariachi music as my assistant would sign to me. I miss my assistant. Chinaland is a mystique. All the trees wear what looks like USC sweaters. There are no people. Only Cadillac cars playing humans playing with cups calling it music. Death to false metal strangles all other statements. Even words go to war. Pomegranate makes the approach. Cadillacs cannot spell. Looking for a panda bear without the use of proper diction. Only short taps for the missing part. Call it parts when expanding the vocabulary. All from the head and the heart. Use long taps for panda signs. The best it did was ask about the rabbit. There is no religion to follow though. This is not acid land. In the here for now I realize that all the Cadillacs run on sugar water. None wear pink shirts with miniature horses playing humans playing with a ball. They call them no people. They all look for a bamboo the panda bear can use. The same Cadillac that was asked comes to me. The singularity is near. That may not have been a question. I speak no words in Cadillac. Do a Russian, take over the scene with nothing but a throwback to protect my feet and ants taking over a Radion. In a past future I recall that navy eyebrows are the best tools for that type of battle.

Chinaland is not just for the China. The panda bear does a search for delicious. A type of music. Plagiarism. On the other side the drums keep the beat. Beats and audio do not mix. Blacks berries and apples too. That was an easy question to Mark. Screaming through the beat of one drum. Roll on by the rest of the drum, way ahead of the curve at this point. The others have a their own side to the situation empty from all learning and screaming. Liars. A version of fortune does a perhaps. Curvy hair trying to curl itself around a head asking to come closer and closer. The talks in Chinaland all sound like music that sounds like drums fading out music. Poetic. It asks you to sing alone only if you speak drum. Sing along if you do not. Fortune favors the brave only in countries like Myanmar. Otherwise fortune will only favor waterboarding. Doing the badap bap bap with all my friends. I remember I do not speak Cadillac. Alone on the hills of Chinaland with a type of no people wearing only USC sweaters. Pants naturally. Sweaters do not really spell out USC. Believe the do not believes and then be set for life. Set on fire too if lucky at all. Pretend your denial is a denial of a denial's denial. Silly goose being in Liam. That was a restaurant. That really was a restaurant. Truthless. The Chinaland secret to cooking is always the spices. No chickens. Back in Myanmar I remember chickens would cluck when no one was looking. Question to Mark is that true question mark. Huness spoke in clucks. I do not remember but I remember he did. The believe is a belief when it becomes common knowledge. Love is all about candy and that gets beliefs going. I can see Pomegranate now playing with the curves of curly. Looks like hair. Red cat. That is why his name was not Robert Paulson. Pomegranate.

They and the gods of small chicken wings

Streets of Chinaland hook you with dropped forks. Still, high the belief and banish all the questions to Mark. No people salesmen peddling to me and to you while I watch me basket with racist drops. Acid drops very fast. Wooden looking containers all red with mosquito bites. Look for the lightly colored ones, they are the best tasting. They said it not me. I have never heard a mosquito speak to me but they said everything to me. Belief in apprehension. Songs about big green monkeys playing in the streets. Maybe only in my head. I am sure I have a head. We can all see the reggae colored notes floating. No drugs involved. The no people will walk. Float on by. None of them looking black. Only racism in the product not the individual. Collective socialist communist communism. I would sell you the pan for free but you, I need you to feed my children and give them coke. One says to Pomegranate. The spirit of the universal Greek still floating in my mind. Paranoia. Perhaps schizophrenia, all natural of course. The sun sets blue in Chinaland.

To the buckle I am it's human. It makes with the hungry. Not the country. I know the correct spelling with no question mark. Not the feeling. Just the junkie impulse of eating. Question to mark, what kind of language does it speak. Question Mark always for the fair and just answers. Suspended from class it tells me. What class, question to Mark. Pretends to be my friend. No curly curves anymore we left it all million miles ahead. Sunset blue means light light. Parading through the air you can still see colors. Buckle, Pomegranate, and me. Band of brothers one and all. Now call it dementia or, still, a simply red. Perhaps kidney failure. A blonde impulse when food appears. Little shop for the little gods. Gods of small chicken wings they call themselves, forgetting the Liam. Huness would love to taste the pictures. No people, only people this time. No USC sweaters. Three personalities folded into one human shape owned by larger panda bears. In Chinaland the gods of small chicken wings are all panda bears. They do a nintendo on the fryers and the chicken wings manage the dance. No quacks, no clucks. Fading spectre of Lola White Cloud and the reason why I was sent here in the first place. I adore her. Love is candy. She had a gummy bear helper. Not a Filipino. Not in 1984 Idaho. The fork will pick itself up as soon as you do. Eating the small chicken wings is not a godly requirement. An atmosphere composed of flip flops and sounds of fading lights. You can hear the here saying the words ugly prima donna. Domestic squabbles with every hare. The gods of small chicken wings smile and give no rabbits for free.

The cavewomen of Chinaland

Streets are filled with cardboard rats all wearing lipstick. Transvestites. Maybe, I would never know. Not anymore. Pomegranate in it's own fantasia. No understanding of sexual orientation. What is sex, question to Mark. Mice dare not tread down the street roads. Elephant playground, the massiveness of a Fantasia situation. Sunset still feels like an umbrella closing, looks like a supernova supernovaing. Lightly lit blue light. You can see the heads of rats coming out of miniature warehouses. They only come out at night, like the red dress. Occasional. Fumble through the sentence fragments looking through the ceiling. Mistake of the aeroplane, looking up when looking forward was the required by and by. Short skirt attention span, rats pay attention to that from the no people. Female question marks exist, question to Mark. Fed and happy the buckle asks to lead into the warehouse. I fear trepidation and sometimes it feels me. I can see the lead rat head.

Too big and too many mushrooms eaten. The Super Mario mistake. Pomegranate corners the smaller of the heads attached to what looks like a body. Fragments it's way into eating it or is Pomegranate eaten by the head rat, another question to Mark. Anxiety but no more salesmen. But there were no salesmen. Black short rats wear scorpions on their right paw. Gang markings no doubt. Doubt everything. They could be blind from the years of lab testing, the boat's whale was right. I forgot my shoes. Silly rabbit. We are outnumbered. Cavewomen pirates appear. The rats flee from a stand dash off and off the stand. There is no standoff. There is no fork. Food was made to heal the moment it was cooked, not when eaten. Everyone knows this, food is dead when cooked. The buckle stead dash fasts itself to my hand. I am it's human. The cavewomen appear with nerves of steel. Magnolia is optional, come only without your ponytails to this fight. They say they will heal this fight. In Chinaland fights are the opposite of a peace treaty. Versailles is a million miles away. Figuratively, of course. Watch for it, later it goes and makes itself ahead. Spatial awareness required. The warehouse feels like it is across a famed Pacific Coast party.

Seek up from caffeine residue. Shock to stop me from doing another faint. My thoughts create their own hum for weight. Anchor is a way. The true way of life. Grammar is all loopholes. The rat with a head, I see, spits out Pomegranate, alive. With my own two eyes it seems I can see. I have only two eyes. Monsters would have more, naturally. Right adjust the water fountains across the gate, seems like a Judge Dredd situation. No Mexican standoffs, this is Chinaland. The cavewomen start to play a music type of jazz. No people cannot do that. Super people, maybe, question Mark but not me. The rats are synaesthetic, the taste of music puts them off buckles and builds their brain squeezed paranoid adrenaline. It is all over the floor. The floor is now all yellow. It tastes yellow too. The floor does. They will all die. The rats, not the floor. They do, Mark. I see the cavewomen doing calisthenics. Celebratory self awareness. The buckle unwraps itself, my hand complains from the swelling the same way a hamster would from overrunning a wheel meant for running, after eating it's own children of course. Only the communist kind of hamsters do that, they also travel the seven seas with whales. Or would the wheel complain about the hamster abusing it. Naturally wheels would not be able to travel the seven seas, they do not speak whale. Thoughts like these are reserved for never situations like this. The master cavewoman comes to me revealing all the coffee shop thoughts that I buried down the well. The well being my brain which has two sides, left and right, never the left. Imagination is somewhere in the middle and in the left is hell. She tells me I am the lion's man and cucumbers my hat. I give her my leopard sunglasses as a form of graciousness. What hat, question to Mark. Emotion flows over the cups. There were no cups. Still liars. Another campfire ridicules me. Gatherings with person piles. Finality of purpose tells me that I will have purpose. I was sent here to save the universe. I pass around my god complex for all to see, along with the buckle. Pomegranate still plays, now with specialist coffee beans for anger management. The cavewoman knew the secret. A single not a plural.

My grandfather the Californian trucker

He never wore a red dress to work. I never had a grandfather, only one. I knew of him and his wearing of black dresses. One piece. Never called himself Cherry but thought of himself as a fine fine thing. This was my conversation with a cavewoman. Ours really. Not hours. There was a purpose of a document. No. Documentation. Discussions and conversations are the slippers you fit getting to know people in. He was born in 1929 to the first sounds of guitar music. This, of course is a parallel timeline. Of course. As a child he was a fortune teller. As an old man he was a Californian trucker. Fountains of trucks under his breath. The gasoline that set the match alight. What they said was that he was never able to pin down the same job for too long. That is what they said. I see Pomegranate not appreciating my spread of words. These were the moments that I opened up my heart. The heart of hearts. Every thing has a heart, even hearts. I see Pomegranate flinching so I launch the belt buckle at it. Hope for a less than friendly situation. Enemies fly at each other. The only reason I would launch the belt buckle. It refused and landed next to cavewomen. Plural not singular in time. What I know of him was his Paul Bunion complexity. The blue bovine was replaced with a black dress. He planted trees when he was older. In his youth he would lonely out all the trees he planted. Killing them. He was a time traveler too. I got his genes. Not his black dresses and none of the hinges. Certainly none of the hinges. I have no hinges.

The first time I met my grandfather he was five. I was a little older. Clap at the thought was the tradition when one told lies. He told me I was a lie. True visionary at that time. He was a carnival. Naturally, he was yet to go back to being his Californian trucker nature. When he had my mom my mom had me. Perhaps the other way around. My grandfather was also the devil. Almost certainly. He was the devil. The age of ten he gave an opportunity to mountain a goat. Her name was Goat Mountain, later to know an Oddball Jack. The mountain goat of course. Gave her land too, later used for amusement parks and suitcase nuclears. The only mountain goat to own a picturesque property. Free from black dresses still. She was also the devil. A story of personality that told many shards. She owned a mall not a mountain. Goat Mountain had a mall, a fighting gift from my grandfather. They fought a lot using words. Sometimes kitchens. A newborn story. Goat Mountain managed the mall made out of glass. Hired several natives to run it for her. They were all goats. Picture perfect specimens that would ask to take the most perfect pictures of themselves. I remember this was the other way around sometime backwards. There was a Garth goat and a suitcase nuclear, again but a singular this time. I hated them, the goats not the remembering. They spoke to me with a unified tangent. I was making things up in my head. I remember seeing them levitate. I swear. The goats. They were all the entire devil too. They made all the pictures in the mall talk. Ending association with my grandfather. Mountain Goat never needed him. He was still the devil without her. Taking to the road in his truck. If asked about the color I only remember the shape. That one was for the spirit of the tiles in my pocket. Exhausted. He still rides to this day somewhere in California. Forever picturing and looking for the next devil. I say all this because we sat in a circle sphere by a lightning fire, not with my grandfather, naturally.

The verbal diatribe would happen by a campfire. I see around me with my looking eyes that we are sitting in what could be described as a mall food court. My eyes came back to own me. Not my sunglasses though. These were gone, naturally. Gone in a less than natural way. Glasses are not natural by nature. Certainly not in the warehouse anymore at least. The glasses, not my eyes. My left hand had abandoned me some time in the future of this past. That was full of rat carcasses dyed in yellow adrenaline. The warehouse, not the future. This was the darkness of the times, perhaps the worst. The best. The leader cavewoman, looking like a patriarch matriarch, would exchange her ideas with me. They would speak without drums. This is all hardcore dusty time. The type of time you find in abandoned food court stories about the first builders of religion. His name was Cicel. He was forty feet tall with a USC shaped body. He started the sweaters, credited for preaching a new pinball religion. Essential degradation and time would see the Cadillacs rise up and own the no people. This was all her, none of me. Even Chinaland had it's own revolutionary. He was a pink Cadillac with the spelled out number printed on its doors. I recall that it was a number but forget the digits. Digitized forgetfulness. She pauses for a second to put more fire on the wood. The fire tastes like rainbow colors and white phosphorous. She tells me fuel for the fire was nerds not woods. She said nerds. A rare currency in Chinaland affecting and appeasing to fires. How do you set fire to nerds, question to Mark. If you look closer you can see all the glasses. They, like the guitars, force their way into my head conversations. Sometimes even in the conversations of conversation of my brain thinker. Grateful for the loss of my glasses, especially the loss of conversation. There were no questions to mark. She was an astonishing creature. She being not Cicel, of course. I had to kill her towards the end, but no reason to mention that. Violence is a currency of appreciation. Violence is the made to heal for Chinaland. Not her, but the residual dust of time around her. I never killed her. I am not college violence. I was not. She tells me with a thick drumming accent how Cicel would count the words he would say every day. True, word, smith. His name was not Smith though, I think. He wrote words for his eyes using a facsimile ear. Philip K. Dick appendages too. Later they were fingers. Not the appendages, not Philip K. Dick. Even appendages can cause confusion. She drums this because in Chinaland there was a Little Californiatown. And of course in Californiatown, Chinaland linguistics come in drum beats. Feels like a long shoreline of incoherency. Though I can hear the see she was saying. A bearded shoreline. Still grateful, they took our troubles away. Her and the beards, naturally done.

Colorblind lighthouses of Little Californiatown

This was a cinnamon colored weekend. Spending some time there can only lead to it being a weekend. Factoid sneaker secrets and short skirts talk to me. Needful. Lola White Cloud haunts my dreams when I sleep. But I never sleep. Exploding brain syndrome. Credit the French navy turning eyeglass insomnia into my natural sport. The giddy dog shines through what I would call my hours. My thoughts take turns deciding to drive and car crash through my brain. Their's too. A controllable trick or treat situation. I wanted to control the trip. Trips are good. Trips are liars. The lead cavewoman would send us on our way for the secret. There was a cloud diverging and needed a song to carry on. Absolute waywardness. Without a sun though. Is it mine, question to Mark. The secret had four legs and owns a panda bear that would own it. Trap door thinking waiting for a messiah to arrive. It was in a lighthouse. Not the secret of course. The panda bear had it's own mule, always behind it, guarding the lighthouse. The Waits conundrum, the seatbelt would add. Incoherent. Capital intonation on visible sounds, the seatbelt calls me brother. A story of another metal verbally masturbating in the eyes of whoever. The panda bear's eyes, not mine of course. I mention this because it can read my thoughts. The panda bear metal, not mine. Pomegranate's red fur by now was a yellowish black. A self blinding loathe of a color. Visibly starting to be a no people. Even cats in Chinaland transform. Michael Bay was deadened. Time to flush it down the toilet, the way of the fish. The Bay not Pomegranate. The rat not Pomegranate. Pomegranate sails through my thoughts, as always. Lies. This would be a diamond hard situation to endure, flushing Pomegranate. The currency of the greatest minds. Lies, not diamonds. Walking past Liam we hear the lead panda bear discussing the tips it received. Not the same guarding the lighthouse. This one battery operated. Chinaland beasts with technology. Monsters. The buckle questions the bear's slippery accent, knowing well that this was not the right bear. My eyes palisade around and through the conversation and the walking, I was waiting for everyone to collect their thoughts. They, naturally, were dragging us all behind.

Our walk electronically squealed. You could tell we were foreign by virtue of sound. Acoustic xenophobia. The sudden road disappeared and rightfully went into a snapping motion. Building up the crescendo to a clapping motion of sound. Roads in Chinaland were synaesthetic, lighthouses were colorblind however. Tables were following, the nose of sound coming from the limbs they called legs. Even sound had smells in Chinaland. The incline of a crescendo is noticeable, even when tables sing it. You can hear the small. Clapping chorus of ahs and ohs. Usual table sounds. Odors too. Less the new car smell. These were the trees of the pavement and followed aliens with snaps crackles and pops. The tables, not the legal aliens. The sun would rise with massive attack. Blitz of mortar fire. Nothing friendly about the bulls. They would launch themselves at every step you take. The tables, not the bulls. Chinaland rises and sleeps with sun wars close to the year 3000.

The crew cut beachhead piano

Red bares all. Resemblance of truth is not true. Not the A Read gummy bears. That was a millennium in the future. Maybe the past. I secret the forgetfulness but remember the options of lighter secrets. Full are they with semi automatics. Is that right, question to Mark. These are Eiffel tower truths all of them, blasting out from muzzles. Insect buzz. Or Arachnids. If there ever was a secret it would have been told already. I can see the flamethrower thoughts that our band was having. Misfits giving birth to the radical. Sounds of phonetics. Currency in Chinaland resembles guitar notes that echo the love and happiness words. Eiffel tower truths were the ones spoken in guitar motifs. Make no mistakes. There is a colorblind lighthouse with the truth, she said that to me. Everyone else said it being heard. The fashion bred truth is that. This was the time to let go of the tiles. The Universal Greek maybe likes that. Even may not. I can see her global concerns slipper away with clicks and clacks of color. At the beach head was a good a place as any. Finally walking down a sand full of hills and beach. No people sailors working for Cadillac boarded ferries. Definitely not on the sand but on the water, of course. Transportation to the future islands of Chinaland. The ferries and not the sand. Construction is the timely displacement. For the beach and not the ferries. The beach has grainy sand. Smooth crystalline faces drawn in each drop, too small for the humane eye. Exactly right for a belt buckle, a colorful feline, and pink tiles belonging to a Mediterranean castaway. Less humane one and all. The beach was a dig stain, looking neon from all the blue the sun threw at it.

Even beaches have heads. Giving heads or having heads, question to Mark. There would be a minimum charge for even that, the usual high five coming from a home called Radio Paradise. The home and not the radio. You can see one of the no people sitting at that head, pretending it was every other appendage locating explanation and meanings of all past lives. The beach's head naturally, not giving head, of course. All the sailors would go there. None have even dared. Brother buckle recalls Alice in Wonderland. The lady sitting with padded slippers centimeters next to a meter of sand for the beach. On the other side of the sand you can see the fluorescence. You cannot. Orange and all the ness. A piano playing what looks like a war drum. More drum speak. Serenade of the bold. Eiffel tower truths seem to mix with Bat dash Man thoughts, remember South America. The lady dressed in all black, but wearing a red dress. Name tag on the dress calling her Cherry. The conversation means to happen and does, Absolut strength of absinth. The impact of the conversation, not the happening. Hey now she would say to our misfits. Cherry would. There is no mark in the question. Not even to Mark. But she speaks in dashes and guitar riffs. Less drums more guitars now. The aeroplane crash plays in my mind, remember what it was like to have it go through me. One day. Perhaps years ago in the distant future. We have the headphone conversation with a pipe to keep company all of the partaking. Cards sitting next to the buckle playing it like a gambling man with a red right hand. Buckles have no hands. Not even cards. But they have an angel demon smile. The evil that cards do. They glow in the dark. Similarly sitting a food's court gathering on the beach's head.

The verbal abuse breaks out with Pomegranate. Not with but through. Visible migraines are the worst, especially when caused by cats. The head of the beach has it. No high fives. Angry cards glowing and a cat, not glowing. Their conversation within a conversation. Discussing the tusk of a rhinoceros is always a type of was debacle. Sides often disagree on their use. Usually disagree on their label. Tusk not a horn. Is a tusk what an elephant would have, question to Mark. The card dialect is filled with dashes, much like Cherry. More drums and sounds that smell however. Her exclusive conversation with me speaks about my grandfather. She knew him. His alcohol fuelled diatribe was driving her drove all the way to Chinaland, on the way to Little Californiatown. Land of dreams and wrong people falling out of cliffs. They came for her in the night of day, forever responsibiling her to this piano. She even points towards it. The piano allows that to happen to make a point about pointing no doubt. Every instrument has a point. Eiffel tower truth. In Chinaland they are also appointed favorable slaves with pipes that do nothing but cum to you. Chinaland panda bears use them as sirens, there was never a Walt or a Disney to describe what kind mermaids should do on the beach. The slaves not the instruments. They came to be meaningful sirens exasperating dialogue and exchanging hats for other discussions. She was also proficient in bullet language, I would learn later.

Still the abdominal pain of a migraine was building requirement for intervention. At some point I had to separate the cards and

Pomegranate, now starting to glow in the dark as well. The fact of interest is Pomegranate's fur changing color with every angry word. Rainbow clown, Pomegranate would start to cease to be. Even cats can make anger. The better part of a rhinoceros was the tusk. The horn depending on the point of view. To such a conversation you have to bring your own light, resourcefully of course. This was a Cosby moment, no more Eiffel tower truths. The humorous legs to sunset pick dash ups move me towards the crowd. Tusks were meant as pick dash me dash ups. Kick starters for the brains and speed for the slower parts of a body. Even Sean Connery knew that, before the sir. Anybody's body even when positioned as a summer home. Being kick starter and not Hollytown celebrities of course. The brain's Avalon is what the cards called it in a fluorescence smell of green. The feline in Pomegranate disagreed, knowing well that it brings with it logic bred thoroughly since the times of Ancient Egyptland. They all died choking on poppy seeds, the lives of Ancient Egyptians. Rapture. Died with dirty hands as well. After confirming the kill, you can see an English sounding accent materializing across the gathering. Seems like a lifetime ago that I heard the same back in the box at the Louvreplace. They all said that, and that was an Eiffel tower truth. The voices. I remember my assistant telling me before we opened a crack case of Rhino Avalon and did a run of sound sniffing. You can tell the aching was worse when the head seasons the beach change, Cherry says. Sandy business even. Translating what the accent meant, Cherry and not the sand of course. Pomegranate was disagreeing. Drive by urge to urinate the words begging for an exit, but that was the piano speaking. It slaps sticks to a bleed out discourse, eight thousand words directly at Cherry. The wreckage that was her life demands she makes weightless logics out of these smelling sounds. Seamless translation. The babel fish of Chinatown. She was the brightest spot on the beach. The piano sparked to life with an almost ruby like sensation. All this time I think, there is no place like home. Where is home, question to Mark.

The piano trepidatiously approaches intent on making up it's own dictionary of words and fire ball abuse. It had a crew's cut. Shape shifting, Cherry explains. The slavery tragedy in her. I mention that she had curly her as well forgetting where I had seen hair anywhere else, or even seen curls that straightened out more than that. Twisted imagery every one hundred thoughts. Everything I thought was wrong. Right then left. Brain thoughts were always the hardest for me to form the Piano says. Through it's babel slave, naturally. Forgive yourself and find the lighthouse it tells Pomegranate before it asks us to leave, bomb strapping the exit with a deviant farm dash. A suspender's moment. Cherry mentions that the Piano speaks in dash. Cherry mentions, not me. Knowing my grandfather more than me, she offers to lay and help with mapping guidance. The best kind of sex is the one on the way to the lighthouse.

She had a lover's touch with a pizza smell

Walking away we realize the maps given were all key chain insignias. Cherry was the love of my life with tender winds she would blow in our ten second sensation. Premature fermentation of a babel slave, not allowed. Though my assistant would have done so with Laika using seasoned space travelling, still loving arms. Hasty. She was the better of the all. No electronica about her, only signals towards the lighthouse. Not Laika. Cherry of course. Mark was always keeping track of the situation, can I blame you, question to Mark. To mention that they were thrown away. His origins I mean. I have to write now, what the lava lamp foetus told me through the warehouse flying home through the year 3000 of 1984 Idaho and into Chinaland. Naturally on the way to Little Californiatown and the colorblind lighthouse. Pomegranate found an accordion playing in it's pockets. Cats do not have pockets. Pomegranate was a kangaroo. Maybe. Explains the bubble crave for vegemite. Always coming to it in fact. I see the vegemite jars dancing around Pomegranate but it tells me that it was the bone dash a dash fide cat. I miss you Pomegranate. Dash speaking Pomegranate. That was Cherry. Not Pomegranate. Confusion in brain accents. Clouded fire breathing minds are usually the curse when your left hand owns the rights. Though I remember finding a lost right hand and adopting it as the left. This was all some Russian time ago.

Pomegranate speaks of ruby slippers missing their owner. Then and not then, of course. They really did smell like pizza. Cherry's did. We were all real, even the piano. It had a head, therefore real.

The emersion of the light case study

You know I can move with the anti visible vibes till now. Considering the inside out of this campus trip across Chinaland for a Little Californiatown. Still walking across the dance dunes looking for inspiration and the secret. On the beach that is. I still pop a vein pill every now and then, walking to the sounds of a reggae function. After leaving that beach that was. Heavy up still. Remember the man in the bird suit getting diseased by his platinum blond mom. That was before the year 3000, probably after. Walking into the light is the way to fool a smart start. I can see the hearing that this is their future island. That was the closer you would get to Little Californiatown. A hemp parade closer by. You would get the same sensation I would get. We were all in the same unison straightening line of a movement. Towards a visible coffee colored grove. Or a groove, question to Mark. Tea colored, coffee was bad and laced with white heroin sugar. With certainly vigour. There was wheat too, along the tea colored coffee streets of course. They all told me that this was a light case study. Not the dark kind. The un heavy kind. A long way in the making. A brave making. The occasional fractal glance into the future remembering a Lola White Cloud and her blade of a mother. I feel safe with you. There would be no mark or dash to dance with.

Always in the approach you would feel the air breathing through the beach head. No longer the head of the beach, that was a while forward now. Disdainful secret, to save a universe of colorful A Read gummy bears, chickens, and roosters tribing their way through 1984 Idaho. The chickens only of course. My assistant would be celebrating his thirty year birthdate about now. Maybe that was then. Not now. Still immersed in a quest for a whisper that would save the world. Really it was all about loving Laika in space. Battery ran out on the buckle. My brother, remembered to be forgotten. We had no time for a proper burial but I afforded a crane burial somewhere on the beach head. It was a yellow crane with spiked wings and a jazz speaking beak. This was before reaching Little Californiatown as well. Temporal insanity.

The celebrity approach this time was neglect. Truthness getting closer to the origin destination. Little Californiatown littered with Garth dash like no people. No Oddball Jack, that was all left behind in the future. Again. One words thoughts for full sentence answers. The likes of Garth I mean. There were wars on a drug happening in Little Californiatown. This was the first immersive case for a study long past the future and due. In time there was no rest of their lives. The cocoa secret, apparently rarer currency there than in most. Run on battles with pigeon nest comfort. No more truths only facts of fiction stabbing through barriers of metaphysical something. You get that same feeling walking into Little Californiatown. This is not a place where you would owe the own. Own nothing in the Little Californiatown, everyone owns everything together. Except for the colorblind lighthouse. Not a light house by any means though. See the albino pundit bears watching the moves around it. Not the same as the panda bears. The wear and tear of time clearly took the toll, removing all color of white and black. Still you can see the a brownish grey though. On the bear not the rocks. Those were historical, the rocks. They were saved for situations just like that. Walking through a street flying with afro bullets. Just like Brazil at a time when there was an Adam West visitation. Singapore that, Pomegranate exclaims.

Half a man drink with water

Little Californiatown was littered with ballroom hair. A result of bullets no doubt. Dancing to a climax that never truly. Walking through with Pomegranate through every other colored building. More dodging than walking. No people use no colors. All have disappeared naturally. The colors. The no people are scared. I am told. In a room with a cell padded to a live perfection. It has been years since I had a drink. Water of course. Perhaps other flavors even. Before that I recall an inquisition moment. Pomegranate relieves itself of question marks in my arms. Just like the Universal Greek said. Lying though, knowing the self messiah. I probably said that, question to Mark. There were the urges that sachet their way through rockets of love. Worse the afro builds. Traversing through all the Garth dash like no people in their none skin suits. Drugs were only allowed in sharp corners. The closest one turns sharply and finds us. Hiding across we see the laws of Little Californiatown plastered letter for letter across every Garth and female Garth. Sometimes even through them. Though Garth may have been a tambourine playing man. Probable being a tambourine playing a man though. Looking across the fullness of the empty room you can see the jar, not full of blond whiskey. This was a soft turn away from the corner. Into a building of course. Naturally done and asking if I ever was a shining soul of a collection. The guard's guard, not the building. I had all the brothers in the buckle. None of the answers however. But really all its asking is if I am real. It also tells me that the died usually prefer graves. I was still thirsty though, years of drinking leading up a magical dysfunction. Just like children singing it hits me over the head and drags the wrong part out to a somewhere.

This was the wrong part of my mind. The one that was dragged. I remember the grand entrance with Pomegranate. Still looking to un secret all of what would save 1984 Idaho, and Lola White Cloud. Her mom was what shaved me. There was a sports bra on the left side right entrance of the lighthouse. The guard's guard dragged us there of course. Unconscious desire does not take you places. It had feelings, the door did. Sounds like a curse of the Irelands, bag pipe fervour. Drunken decadence and eclectic fornication, a wonder the lighthouse went blind Pomegranate tells me. On the way through the left side entrance where you can see elephant marks of colors pumping fists and jetpack animosity all through the atmosphere. That after the heavy sighs of the door at that I can see were ties roped to my hands. The panda bears were out to lunch, more gods of small chicken wings for everyone. Perhaps how color was lost, question to Mark. Things would have been messy otherwise. They were still messy, naturally. In the nature of things as it were. On the way through the elevator, you can hear someone walking up the stairs inside. Elevator conversation, really a habitual mind fuck. You can also hear the facts blurting out of what I thought was a camera but was a speaker. In the corner of the elevator you would have seen a Mozambique situation brewing. There was a tan sensation electrifying what was breathable air. The facts the elevator was spewing. Eiffel tower truths again describing animals at birthday parties flying the high seas. Pirating even. Discussions between hamsters, lonesome drawing boards, whales, and the sort. I remember they were boat's whales even. This was an afro situation, much like the made up bullets of a past future hour. For a moment I remember how Angy would blow. She blew truth. Not the true true coming from an Atlas driven cloud. Ritalin explosions through the door. The truth, outing in there we thought.

Even close to a thousand words said per minute per minute you could still stay thirsty. I still was despite the speed of talk and run. I would have disembodied for a salad. Perhaps I did. The elevator was pregnant with violent mystique. Mine. This would be the point that directs to a sign indicating an un secret. The last thing you heard walking out of the elevator was zombies are the only people that can fly. That was true enough for the birth of a messiah complex. I wish my assistant was there to see it. Colorful antennas paining their way through the doors. Loudly even.

Birds carnivore through life

Carefully planned irony would atmosphere its way through me and Pomegranate. It was a less than tank solution, digging through trenches across the room of cartoonish panda bears. The doors would open themselves with a chuckle, their currency was kittening the situation. That was before the trenches though. Doing just that, I remember all of this was to save the Laundromat society that was 1997. Digging the trenches I mean. What I could never tell was through all the follow dash up suites and sweet juice they gave me, they were all dying to live. The panda bears. I suspect everything reached the climax, but most likely why my question marks were taken away from me. Pomegranate was climaxing for a last breath. There was an erection on the wall, right in front of the elevator door. I felt rhyming sympathy and a mixture of malice. Knowing well that throwing Pomegranate the second first through the door was a mistake. Naturally, throwing was reserved for buckles and not cats. You can still hear the harmonica in Pomegranate's pockets, reading poetry out loud. Sometimes topping the Lola White Cloud dreams that have me. An accordion sounding ice cream dream. He climaxed with seductive birthmark music impaling through erection wall impact. My grandfather remembered then, in a wrinkly manner telling me to always walk backwards into a violent room. I remembered, not my grandfather of course. The top of the lighthouse was darkly violet. Color of violent. Taste is not a requirement for a colorblind linguistic. Especially if it was a light house. Turning around the memory meant learning the difference between a lightening step and a lightning step. That was a lightening step, naturally. You could see the bird at the arm's length. It would later explain that it was eighty three years old hiding in a lighthouse cage.

In Chinaland time was a fearful thing. Panda bear phobia. The bird was big and yellow though. Not yellow, hot blue color cooling through the vision eyes. Seems yellow from the lack of blue sun. This was real, question to Mark. Plausibly what happens next dampens Pomegranate's accordion sounding harmonica. The bird would teleport it's violence from sleep to awake, yelling for attention. The room would build with fearsome air, like pants waiting to be fully ironed in an instant. You can see the color change to gold at this point. Panda bear extinction. Beautiful. The bird possibly ate Pomegranate. Or did I, question to mark. I found my thoughts shuffling into a dash hopeful dash accent crushing down what can only be described as my brain. You have never a seen a bird carnivore it's way through a cat.

Film sachets and transport

A peaceful color later, I realize the bird was bald. It's voice sounding like a tone of rings. I can still hear it blink. It's eyes. Not the voice of course. The savior of 1984 Idaho was an enflamed hole shaped like a

Frank Doz Jr. bird. More like a cartoon version however. A squinting tweety bird. We had a weekday discussion all through. Teaching time how to reverse itself and me looking to come home. Explaining it's age and the information on all flightless birds I came to understand the secret. Using exactly six words repeated three times without any numbered numbers. The bird owned a film sacheting it through into Little Californiatown. Patiently waiting for it to off the show, I dropped kicked it the film box, crashed through the lighthouse window and found myself home. It told me to.

Instead of the usual crash to the ground I saw a red haired portal swallow me. Thinking that the box would save Lola. My dear Lola. Nothing like Cherry or the cavewoman. All lies. The box gratefully accepted by the ground, disappeared. Crushing sounds and headphones, the point where things got hard. Someone put a dress on me reversing blood flow while caressing a certain handicap. The moment to which I faint. The box ran away, finding its way back to 1984 Idaho. Perhaps. You all have me here, my attention divisibly dividing. I wonder how the bird is, question to Mark.

I have had a box with time in it. I do not know. I have no punctuation. I am tired. My world did stop in 1997; I can see it staring at me, before all my travels. Mean stare. All I can do was try to save it, the world of course. It would still stare. Poke it in the eye to blink. Was there a Stand Ford, question to Mark. Your padded thoughts keep me here, on basis tempo rare. I was in Stand Ford, and perhaps fifty years. In the fifty years, not about them. Or may be ago. Ago come and leave, classy event you all. This was a time traveling adventure thirty years in experience. Making promises too. It really could be too late. Answering your questions I will tell you this, Mark. I was always from a Sunday and I can read you.